MORNING

SONG

BY

SHARON LEE BEATTY

Purple Unicorn Press, July 2016

ISBN 978-0-692-64540-6

Typeset in Trajan Pro by Carol Twombly at Adobe and Palatino by
Hermann Zapf at Linotype

www.purpleunicornpress.com

For my grandchildren

"I know how birds fly, fishes swim, and animals run... But there is the dragon — I cannot tell how he mounts on the winds, through the clouds, and rises to heaven..."

— *Confucius*

Chapter One

There is a legend about the dragon, Shi-lin. They say she died of a broken heart.

* * *

Kimi was hurrying to finish her Aunt's errands. Her final stop was the apothecary's shop to buy Grandfather's medicine when she heard someone call her name. *Fàng pì!* Not Mei. And not today when Kimi had so much on her mind.

Mei stormed down the stone-slab street as fast as her heavily pregnant body and tight skirt would allow. Her cheeks, flushed with the late August heat, complemented her perfect skin. Even the elaborate hair arrangement sat perfectly underneath her heirloom headdress.

Kimi's own brown cotton skirt and hastily woven braid were more appropriate for the market and the long walk to and from Kaisun. Mei's fussy clothing and hairstyle did not impress Kimi one bit. Especially since the girls had known one another all their lives.

Kimi considered the possibility of escaping back into Kaisun's market. She never knew what to expect from the magistrate's daughter. Sometimes Mei behaved as sweetly as she had growing up. Other times she was an insufferable, gloating *chui niu bi*. It started when Mei married and it worsened with pregnancy. What happened to the girl who used to sneak into the backyard of the mean baker's house to collect tadpoles in his creek?

Mei stopped within an arm's length of Kimi with her hands on her hips, nose in the air. "Did a messenger of the gods reveal your special destiny yet? Has your grandfather said anything to you about a husband? Has your Aunt Lu seen the matchmaker? Oh, I forget; they aren't your real family, are they?"

Kimi reached for the medallion around her neck. Sometimes it lent her patience. Though Mei never seemed to care when they were children, now she pointed out Kimi's foundling status whenever she could. According to Mei, foundlings were relegated to the lowest rungs of society, especially girls.

As for her special destiny… Kimi wished she had never mentioned her mother's letter or the medallion left with her. The course of someone's life couldn't be known when she was still a baby. She had control of her future. If she married an unkind man, she'd misbehave until he was forced to send her back.

"The matchmaker hasn't come, but Grandfather has written letters." The statement was certainly true. He wrote many letters, and some of them might be about a husband. At seventeen, Kimi was already old for marriage. She didn't care. Marriage didn't matter as long as she could open her school.

Kimi had things to do—a life to live that might or might not include a husband.

Mei leaned toward Kimi's ear, brushing her full belly against Kimi's arm, and whispered, "I'll bet your grandfather will find you a desperate, old, pig farmer to marry. Someone with a spiteful mother and a drunken brother. That will be your special destiny. Pig farmer's wife." Mei giggled.

Kimi turned and took several steps towards the apothecary's shop. Mei followed on Kimi's heels.

Kimi clamped her fists to her side. Girls just didn't punch each other. Kimi tried to think wholesome thoughts about Mei's idyllic life—a kind, tolerant husband, a baby the midwife swore would be a boy and not a useless girl, and considerable wealth— but she couldn't resist hoping that terrible things would happen to Mei.

"I know. It won't be a pig farmer," Mei said. "It will be a river man, and he'll sell you to a foreign sailor for a sack of rice. You can recite the classics while you scrub his ship."

"At least I know the classics. I can have meaningful conversations with my husband, if I ever have one. I'm not a silly ornament." Kimi's cheeks flushed with heat, but she didn't regret the angry words no matter how rude. Maybe one day a girl wouldn't need a husband in order to have a good life.

Deep lines appeared at the corners of Mei's mouth. "You are a hopeless dreamer, Kimi. Even if you had a husband, and even if he agreed to let you start a school for girls, do you think anyone would come? It's not natural. What use are the writings of the great scholars when your son has a fever?"

Kimi put her hands on her hips and leaned into Mei's face. "Then why not shop for plain cotton for your new skirts? Cotton skirts will cover you nearly as well, and they are less expensive."

Mei's perfect eyebrows pulled together. "What does that have to do with teaching girls?"

"Everything," Kimi growled. "Money is good for more than buying silk."

Mei's ivory cheeks flared red. "I can see that having no mother to raise you has made you a mannerless ape."

How dare she bring up my mother! Kimi felt her mouth pull back, baring her teeth. Her fists clenched so tightly they tingled, growing warm as if she'd been holding them before a fire.

Color drained from Mei's cheeks. Her eyes grew round as she took a step back.

"And you are a spiteful fox," Kimi said, leaning forward. She wanted to say more, but first one and then another woman raced by.

The tailor's wife ran up to them. "Mei! Kimi! Come! Lanfen saw a dragon."

Kimi's spell of anger broke, leaving her dizzy for a moment. Her hands cooled as the blood seemed to drain from them.

Mei's eyebrows were pushed so high, they almost disappeared, but as the woman ran past, her eyebrows fell quickly. Mei's eyes twinkled with the signs of adventure Kimi remembered from their youth. She grabbed Kimi's arm, drawing her back into the center of the street to follow the herald to the women's gathering place in front of the laundry.

So like Mei—friends when convenient. Kimi shrugged off her grip.

More women rushed by—a bright stream of red, yellow, and aqua skirts under brown padded jackets with upright Mandarin collars.

The voices in the street grew louder, the pitch higher, as the women's excitement built. Shouts of "Dragon" from a dozen more racing women echoed off the brick buildings.

Kimi's heart beat to the sound of each shout. She would bet every hairpin she'd ever own that whatever it was, it wasn't a dragon. But it had to be something interesting to attract this much attention.

Several businessmen poked their heads out of their doorways, taking that moment to sweep their doorsteps while others shook their heads and went back inside. It would be undignified for men to show any interest in women's gossip, but Kimi suspected they would ask their wives to recount every detail.

Mei shouted over her shoulder at Kimi: "A dragon! Can you imagine it? In Kaisun? What do you say now, Kimi?"

Kimi bit her lip. She would know soon enough. Hiking up her skirt, she followed Mei down the narrow street, aiming for the raucous gabble ahead. They dashed past the dried geese that hung beside the meat shop door, their late-afternoon shadows stretching long in front of them. Racing past the shoemaker's cubbyhole, she wrinkled her nose at the odor of tanned leather, glimpsing rows of brightly colored shoes as she hurried on.

Twenty or so women were gathered in a tight circle in front of the laundry. They talked over one another, their voices a patchwork quilt of sound.

"…north…"

"…she did too say…"

"…it was black…"

"…dragon…"

Kimi and Mei wedged themselves between women and shopping baskets before the crowd separated them. Kimi worked her way toward the center where Lanfen, the short, fat tinker's wife, stood on a box.

"I swear it was a dragon," a woman shrilled.

Another woman waved her hand. "You drank too much rice wine, Ahn."

The tight energy of the crowd sizzled like pork in hot oil. This wasn't the usual wringing of hands and lamenting over ungrateful children, inconsiderate husbands, troublesome neighbors, and all the ailments and pain that women suffer.

Kimi could see the glint of their eyes as the speakers checked the crowd around them to be sure they had everyone's attention.

A piercing voice cried over the buzz. "What does it mean?"

"Famine," a deep voice said with conviction. It was Tsu, the broad woman with the soaked apron who worked the laundry and carried an acrid cloud of lye around her like bad incense. Kimi never paid the laundress much attention. She was the most superstitious of Kaisun's women and by far the biggest gossip.

"The dragon will dry up our rivers and make it so that the clouds give no rain," Tsu said.

Another voice shouted, "I dreamed of a great funeral. The Empress will die. Shang Ti, the God of Gods, will come for her. I saw his chariot drawn by four phoenixes. And my dreams are always true."

Dragons riding the seas and air? Drawing water from the heavens? Bringing famine or floods? Pah, as Aunt Lu would say. *Fàng pì!* Even the lowliest of modern nineteenth-century scholars knew that drought was a matter of weather cycles, not magic.

So, what did the women really see? There would be some kernel of truth at the root of the stories, but it would be something with a sensible explanation.

Mei pushed her way back to Kimi's side, drawing her attention away from the women's gossip. "See? There are dragons. Oh, I forgot. You don't believe in magical creatures, do you Tengshe? You don't believe in Shang Ti, Kuan Yin, or Lord Yama, either, right? They aren't modern enough."

She hated it when Mei called her by her birth name. It was a secret. "You're right. I don't believe in magical creatures and I doubt there are gods, at least not ones who walk among us in disguise making judgments on people. Think about it, Mei. If there were gods, why not have them settle arguments in front of the magistrates? We could call on the gods and receive wise rulings that everyone would accept. Why let bad rulers live?"

"That's not how it works, Kimi. We are lucky the gods pay attention to us at all."

"I can't conceive of two worlds—one in the clouds and one down here. The one up there full of magical beings flying around doing impossible things and popping down here from time to time to interfere in human lives."

"You don't even believe in dragons or evil spirits. You're silly, Kimi."

"No, you're the one who's silly."

Mei looked down her superior nose. "Tell me you don't feel your spirit inside of you sometimes. Mine talks to me and makes me see the beauty in things. Sometimes I can feel my grandmother's spirit reach out from the heavens to comfort me. So where do these spirits go when we die? I can see that people who were murdered would want to take over somebody else's body to wreak the vengeance that compels them. They pervert the spirit of the living person, turning them into wicked spirits."

Mei rubbed her belly and looked up the hill toward her home. "The gods better help us. A dragon is terrible news. I need to tell my husband's mother." Mei's skirt rustled as she hurried away.

Kimi wiped the late afternoon heat from her brow and turned her attention back to the crowd, hoping to hear what really happened.

She let the sounds wash over her, listening as the voices became louder and louder. War. Fire. Flood. Famine. Death. A dozen wild foretellings.

Near her, Mrs. Xie spoke in a low voice, "No, it wasn't a dragon. It was a black crane, I tell you. Black neck, black head, black tail, and black feet—there among all the white ones."

"I didn't see anything," Zhi said. "No dragon. No crane."

Kimi smiled, feeling vindicated. Ah, yes! The kernel of truth has been discovered. Only an unusual bird. Not a dragon.

Aunt Lu dreamed of a black crane two nights before. She made dire prognostications, sure that a black crane warned of terrible things to come. Certainly an odd coincidence, her aunt dreaming of a black crane and Mrs. Xie seeing one. Perhaps it flew by the lake and Aunt Lu forgot, assuming it was a dream.

Oh, *Fàng pì!* Aunt Lu would gloat for days about the black crane.

* * *

Kimi backed away from the gaggle of gossiping women and turned towards the apothecary's shop to complete her aunt's last errand.

Relieved at the coolness of the small shop, Kimi lay her satchel down on the ancient wooden counter. The rust-brown shoulder bag bulged with the week's mail—thick letters addressed to the Honorable Wang. Her grandfather would be excited to find two books from America included among the letters, newspapers, and journals. The magistrate's clerk had handed them to her as though the detested foreign books would sprout tiger fangs and bite his hand off.

"Good morning, Mister Chin." Kimi turned to point toward the street. "Have you heard the rumors about a reported dragon sighting?"

"I have two ears and two eyes; of course I know. Such carrying-on." Kaisun's herbalist brushed the subject aside with his hand.

He was a tiny man, with walnut skin hanging loosely from spindly arms and dark spots marbling his cheeks and forehead. His scraggly white beard narrowed to a point above his heart. He had seemed just as old when Kimi had started coming into town for the mail when she was seven.

"What will it be today, Kimi?"

"Grandfather needs more medicine. And Aunt Lu suggests it be a bit stronger."

Mister Chin frowned and stroked his beard. "Has he not been sleeping?"

Kimi shook her head. "Only an hour or two, and he barely eats. I can see the pain imprinted on his face as clearly as one of his calligraphy paintings."

"He will be visiting Lord Yama soon," Mister Chin said.

Mister Chin had it wrong. Grandfather wouldn't go anywhere near the death god, because there was no death god.

Mister Chin turned to the wall with its floor-to-ceiling case of herbs and medicines arrayed in jars of varying sizes and colors. His skinny arms reached to the top of the narrow shelves where he lifted a large glass jar filled with golden powder. He set it on the counter as carefully as a mother laying her newborn baby in its cradle. As he opened it, the familiar smell of rotten eggs burst from the jar. So many times she had watched him prepare her grandfather's medicine. She knew every ponderous step.

"Do you have news for Grandfather?" Mister Chin spoke little but heard much from the merchants, farmers, and fish sellers coming through Kaisun. Her grandfather relied on Mister Chin's judgment regarding which rumors had substance.

"The grocer heard from the fish sellers that Japanese ships were seen on the Yalu River, not far from Dandong," he said.

A touch of fear tingled down Kimi's back. "Right off our coast? Do you think they'll cross over from Korea? We're too big for them to swallow with their hungry mouths, aren't we?"

"Perhaps." Mister Chin tapped the little silver thimble until the yellow powder was level, and then poured it into the mouth of the waiting brown bottle. He shook the bottle eight times—always eight times—sealed it and handed it to her.

Kimi placed three coins on the counter.

Mister Chin slid them into his pocket. "Does your grandfather continue with your studies?"

Kimi lifted her head. Though more open-minded than most, Mister Chin believed in the old ways. He indulged her, but that was all. Still, she was proud of her grandfather for teaching her things only boys from gentle homes learned. "When he's able to. He's teaching me to read the English newspapers from Shanghai."

Mister Chin shook his head, betraying a small smile. "I cannot say I think it's wise to give you a young scholar's education."

Kimi stretched her neck as high as it would go. "Someday China will learn women are good for more than making sons. Maria Mitchell was a great astronomer who started a college for women. I want to be like her."

Mister Chin laughed. "You have told me about your Maria and her comets. Perhaps the gods will send one—a long-tailed *tui xing* to strike retribution on our Empress."

Kimi almost corrected him. Angry gods didn't send comets. They were planetary bodies like stars and planets with predictable orbits. But even open-minded Mister Chin wouldn't agree.

Kimi tucked the bottle into her satchel, making space for it beside the books so that it stayed upright. After a proper bow to Mister Chin, Kimi turned her steps towards home.

Kimi went behind the crowd of gabbling women. They'd be at it for hours.

As she passed the bakery, Mister Cho, the fat proprietor, was swinging his broom and shouting at three small boys playing in the street in front of his shop. He didn't like children; his loudest and rudest shouts he reserved for his nephew—a little boy named Hachi. Small for his six years, and generally quiet, Hachi was the center of today's game. Mister Cho didn't like women, either. Aunt Lu said his wife left him shortly after they married. Kimi would have, too.

She turned her back to him and kept walking.

Evening shadows painted the ground, and dust rose from the wide, dirt road as she made her way downhill. Moist air, cooled by the lake, blew stray hairs into her face. She brushed them back. The breeze loosened them again, so she gave up.

The red glow of sunset filled the valley, making the mountains in the distance appear to be on fire. She loved this peaceful time of day. As she paused the world seemed to take a deep breath and calm itself. Rumors of war with Japan faded to nothing.

Everything seemed possible. Her dreams would be as easy to grasp as the early star hanging low over the hills. She could choose her own destiny. Her husband's voice would be as gentle as the song of the cranes. She would make a school where girls were eager to learn history, debate the classics, and explore the strange new European ideas and with a library so big she could read every day and never read the same words twice. She could imagine a million things.

She imagined her mother as a beautiful woman brought low by circumstances. Aunt Lu didn't know anything about Kimi's family. She'd found baby Kimi on the doorstep with a simple note. "Take care of her, for I cannot. I have named her Tengshe—one who soars. Destiny has placed its hand on her soul. The Goddess has touched her heart. Tell her I love her and not to be afraid of who she is."

Nothing else but the note and the medallion with a dragon curving around the pearl in its claws. She hid the name and the prophecy from others, except Mei, but she wore the medallion. It calmed her when she was vexed, reminded her to be strong when she felt the world was against her, and gave her courage when she had nightmares.

She might not believe in dragons, but her mother was real, wherever she was. Her mother's life must have been hard if she gave up her baby.

When Kimi reached the lake road, she looked toward the mountains north of Kaisun and saw only wispy clouds and the rosy glow of the setting sun reflected off the ridges.

And as she expected, no black crane and no dragon.

Chapter Two

Shi-lin was born on a day when the sun did not rise from the east as it should, but arrived midday from the back of the moon. The elder dragons excused her odd behavior because of the strangeness of the heavens at her birth.

When the dragon children traveled the seas, as young dragons do, she lagged behind to watch the ships and the men scrambling along the rigging as they set their sails.

When other dragon girls played among the clouds, hoping to catch glimpses of the gods, Shi-lin peered toward the earth, watching the men labor in their fields.

When she was grown, she spent long days cloaked with invisibility, listening in the markets of the cities.

She loved the people of China. There was symmetry in the cycles of their short lives, honor in their devotion to one another, and beauty in the things they made. For many years, she walked beside them unseen and learned their ways.

* * *

Kimi continued along the road that hugged the lake to the hollow between three birch trees on the shore. She was close enough to see her house if she peered through the leaves, but no one could see her. It was her hiding place when she wanted to be alone. Soon it would be too cold, even if she nestled under a mound of blankets. Winters in Manchuria were harsh, even in the southern part where they lived.

Focused on her thoughts, she barely noticed the traveler until he stopped in front of her gate. Grandfather wasn't expecting a visitor. He would be delighted to have a guest. Still, he would stay up late into the night, compromising his already frail health.

The man stayed by the gate and watched as she approached, brushing the leaves from her skirt.

Why was he waiting for her? How did he even know she lived here?

As she neared the gate, a trick of the light made the man seem immensely tall beside a walking staff the size of a tree. She blinked. He was just a slender stranger covered with dust from the road with a faint odor of earth and dry leaves about him.

She bowed to him, holding the bag with Grandfather's medicine and mail close to her side. He returned the courtesy. Then he stepped forward, golden light illuminating his face. A young face—too young to wear the gold button on the top of his scholar's cap. He was a prodigy, then, to pass the highest exam before lines had settled on his face. His wide-set, gold-flecked eyes sparkled in the waning sunlight.

"Hello, Kimi." He shared the warm smile of a friend.

Who was he? The arching brow and the unusual eyes seemed familiar, but she couldn't place the narrow face or the low, resonant voice.

"Honored Scholar, I apologize, but I don't recall your name."

"I am Long Xiao. It's been many years." His voice sounded as smooth as a muffled bell.

"Xiao?" He'd lived with her family for five years and been like an older brother to Kimi. She searched his face for signs of the fourteen-year-old boy she'd known. She probably had changed as much; she'd been only eight when he'd left to continue his training in Mukden.

He was taller; face longer; no more the plump, round face she remembered. What surprised her most was his stillness. Even his eyes were still, seeming to see all of her in that steady gaze. Not even a twitch of his long fingers on the staff. She'd never seen such calmness in a person. His smile began deep within and shone through his eyes.

Noble. That's what came into her mind. Great depths of wisdom. His thoughts and words seemed imbued with weighty meaning. He was a man now, not the boy who had played with her in the woods. What else had changed about him? She wondered how he saw her.

His eyes glowed as he studied her. "You have grown to be a beautiful, young woman. Does life please you?"

What could she say? She certainly wasn't beautiful. Did life please her? Although she studied science with Grandfather and read a lot, her other accomplishments were trivial. He had been to the Imperial City. He had passed the ordeal of his exams. She had her dreams, but so far had done little to begin them. How would Xiao react when he heard of her plans? It didn't matter what he thought. Straightening her shoulders, she said, "I am content."

He nodded politely. "And your grandfather. He is well?" Xiao's voice didn't sound so deep now, and his face wasn't as smooth. Little creases appeared in the corners of his eyes.

He would see for himself shortly, but she could prepare him. She patted her bag. "I'm bringing his medicine. I don't think he will live much longer. He's weak. The pain is terrible, though he never complains."

Xiao's eyes darkened as he listened. It seemed that she could look right through them to see inside. Sorrow. "I have come in time, then."

"He'll be glad to see you." She nodded toward his hat. "Especially when he sees that you passed your exams."

Xiao cocked his head to one side. "And you, Kimi? Are you pleased?"

He kept his eyes focused on her as if he wanted a real answer, not the usual polite words one says without thinking. The moment seemed too slow, as though the future of China hung on her next sentence. She blinked and banished the strange mood. He wasn't a mysterious stranger. His words weren't dripping with hidden meaning. She had played with him. She had seen him covered in mud after losing his balance and sliding down the hill behind the garden. He'd seen her on the kitchen floor covered in pickle juice and broken pottery. He was probably here to show Grandfather the brilliant scholar he'd become.

"Yes," she said. Certainly his success mattered, and not just because he'd been Grandfather's student. They'd been best friends, but she was no longer the small child who'd followed him around like a shadow. She hoped he didn't still see her that way. She turned to hide her sudden embarrassment.

The gate opened smoothly at her touch, the wood warm with the afternoon sun. Stepping inside, the faint scent of pine rose as her feet crushed the matted needles on the path. Ordinary smells. Nothing mystical. Only a reminder that the courtyard needed to be swept.

The ginger cat waiting outside the gate rubbed against Xiao's legs with a soft, "Mrrow." Years before, Xiao had helped her save the kitten from the market where it would have been caught, raised without care, and then sold to the butcher for a few coins.

He scooped up the cat with one arm and tucked it against his chest, and with that familiar movement, the hint of a spell broke. He was just Xiao. He followed her through the gate, his steps falling softly on the stones of the courtyard, his staff tapping as softly as his steps.

The setting sun threw his shadow ahead of him. The odd feeling returned. His shadow covered the walkway before her and climbed the wall of the house. She wore his shadow like a comforting blanket wrapped around her. She blushed. Not at all a proper thought for a big brother who had come home.

* * *

Carrying the mail and the fresh bottle of medicine, Kimi headed down the hall to Grandfather's room.

Xiao followed her. "May I come with you to see your grandfather?"

Fine. But first she had to prepare him for this surprise. "I'm sure you want to wash yourself and eat dinner first. I won't be long. I'll tell him you are here."

Kimi took several steps forward, assuming Xiao would go to the kitchen. Instead, he looked at her in a way that took in the whole of her. Kimi blushed, wishing he would go visit Aunt Lu so she could spend a few minutes with Grandfather.

He smiled the smile he had when they were children. "I could help you carry the mail."

If only he would quit staring at her! "No. He might be napping. If not, I can prepare him for your visit."

Xiao nodded in understanding and turned toward the kitchen. Even though he no longer watched her, she felt his eyes on her the whole way to Grandfather's room.

She entered quietly so she wouldn't disturb him if he were dozing. He looked up from the bed where he leaned against the headboard. A thin round pillow propped behind him protected his bony spine from the carved ridges of his headboard—another dragon. He had pushed down the dinner tray to make room for the leather-bound book filling his lap.

The light from the oil lamp on the bedside table accentuated the deep lines illness and age drew around his eyes and on his forehead. Hollows curved his long cheeks, ending at the thin line of his mouth.

He removed the glasses perched on the end of his small nose. With age-gnarled hands, he folded the earpieces and set them aside. His quick smile didn't camouflage the pain shadowing his eyes.

Kimi set the mail and newspapers on his desk and the new books and the bottle of medicine beside his glasses on the bed table. The books were in English—a language he'd recently mastered, at least in written form. Her fingers trailed over the pressed leather spines, eager for him to finish reading them so they could discuss the merits of English wisdom.

She lifted the dinner tray from his lap. "Grandfather, you haven't eaten your dinner again. How will you get better if you don't eat?"

He dismissed her comment with a hand wave. "I will ask my sister to prepare something if I am hungry later."

Kimi shook her head. She knew he wouldn't.

"Do we have a visitor?" he asked. "I thought I heard a stranger's voice coming from the front of the house."

"Yes, Grandfather. Xiao has come to visit." She arranged her face so he wouldn't see the concern written there. He wouldn't sleep, and to stay alert he wouldn't take his medicine.

She said nothing. A dutiful daughter didn't burden her elders with worries.

"Xiao," he said, leaning back into his pillow and closing his eyes. His shoulders had dropped their usual tension. She thought for a moment he had fallen asleep. Sometimes he did that—fell asleep in the middle of a thought. But he opened his eyes again and nodded slowly. This time his smile was fuller and less strained, his back straighter.

Perhaps Xiao's visit would be good, assuming he didn't stay too long. "Did you expect him?"

"I received a letter a month ago and hoped he would come. If he is not too tired, I would like to see him tonight. Did you know he has been admitted to the Empress's court?"

Pride swelled through Kimi. "That's wonderful news. I'm sure he'll want to see you right away. Once Aunt Lu is done feeding him, that is."

He nodded again. "I can wait. I will take only half of my medicine now."

She reached for the pitcher and filled the pale green porcelain cup half full of water. At least he was taking some of his medicine. Her heart wept to see him in so much pain. As tempting as it was, she didn't give him the full dose. That would violate his trust. She added one measure of medicine and stirred it with the measuring spoon before handing it to him.

His nose wrinkled at the faint smell of rotten eggs. Still, he drank the medicine without complaint.

"What news from town today?" he asked.

She poured another cup of water which he sipped slowly as she organized her thoughts. How much should she tell him? He was old and sick and now he had a visitor. He needed his rest, not complications. Xiao would probably tell him about the growing unrest and the rumors that both Japan and Russia were taking far too much interest in their quiet corner of China. But Xiao might not know about the Japanese ships. She should tell Grandfather that much. This would concern him. Grandfather didn't trust the Japanese to honor the recent treaty with Korea. In fact, he didn't trust Japan.

"Grandfather, Mister Chin heard from the grocer that Japanese ships were seen on the Yalu River, near Dandong."

His mouth formed a thin line. "How long ago was this? Did he say?"

"I don't know. The grocer heard it from the man who brings him fish."

"How often does the fish come?"

"Twice a week."

"So the news is no more than a few days old." His eyes had a faraway look. He took a deep breath and turned his attention back to her. "Any other news?"

"Nothing except women's gossip," she said. "Lanfen says she saw a dragon. Mrs. Xie said she saw a black crane. The women think it means a disaster is coming."

One corner of his mouth turned up. "Perhaps there will be change, but not because of a dragon. Have you told my sister yet?"

By the twinkle in his eyes, Kimi could almost guess what he would say next.

"If I know my sister, she'll have this house upside-down in a matter of days."

Kimi grimaced. That's what she was afraid of.

He nodded in the way that meant the conversation was over. She stood and picked up the shawl draped over the foot of the bed. It would be a chill evening. Maybe no frost yet, but soon.

He patted her hand as she wrapped the shawl over his shoulders. "Send Xiao when he's rested, Daughter."

When he called her that, it didn't matter she was a foundling. It made her heart smile.

"Yes, Grandfather. I will."

He picked up the green book again. As she left, his fingers began to trace the lines crossing the page.

* * *

Xiao stepped aside as Kimi entered the kitchen with the tray. He was fresh with the dewy gleam of wet hair. His black housecoat had a silk border embroidered in red and gold dragons. Dragons, again.

"Is your grandfather ready for me?"

"Yes, but please don't keep him up too late, and give him another dose of his medicine before you leave." Kimi realized she sounded like a scolding mother.

"I will take good care of him."

Kimi watched his smooth glide as he walked down the hall. No, he was no longer the impatient boy darting through the hallways.

* * *

Kimi ate a dumpling while Aunt Lu laid out dishes for the next morning's meal and rambled on about this and that, mentioning people Kimi barely knew. The men's voices hummed quietly from the back of the house.

She took small nibbles around the edges of the bun, saving the sticky, spiced meat hidden in the center for the last bite. Fortunately, her aunt was too busy preparing for breakfast to notice her breach of manners.

"*Pah!* Let that be a lesson to you," Aunt Lu muttered as she poured a scoop of rice into a pot.

Oh, no. Not another lecture on the proper behavior for a Chinese woman. Aunt Lu lived in an old-fashioned world. Women still believed in the superstitions and legends they'd been raised with. She insisted that each one told a lesson. To her, they were her legacy to Kimi. The number four was bad luck, but eight good luck. You weren't supposed to clip your nails at night or sweep for three days after the New Year—all to keep ghosts away. The old stories were fine for Aunt Lu, but the world was different now.

"… Not that the old widow Shikai doesn't deserve it, treating her daughter-in-law like a slave, but this time the daughter went too far. *Pah!* Nothing good will come of it. If the son has to stop the feud, it will be the wife who loses, not the mother." She looked sternly at Kimi then went back to measuring rice. "The girl's nose is so high it is a miracle she doesn't drown when it rains."

While her aunt's long face seemed intent on her meal preparations, her mind focused on the lesson. The lessons were given with affection and with Kimi's wellbeing in mind, but they grew tiresome. She made a small sound—enough to let Aunt Lu think she was listening then let her mind drift, wishing she could be part of the men's discussion where she could learn something useful.

Aunt Lu shook her head as she replaced the lid on the rice bucket, making the knot of her gray hair wobble. She reached up with her long, skinny fingers to tighten the pin that held it in place. Aunt Lu might not be pretty—way too skinny and her features too plain—but she cared about her appearance and rarely had even a single hair out of place, unlike widow Shikai.

Kimi empathized with the young wife. If Kimi had to wash clothes again and again, she would have rubbed dirt into the widow's favorite shirt. If her husband wouldn't defend her, she'd go back to her family even if it meant disgrace.

She couldn't share those thoughts with Aunt Lu. If she did, her aunt wouldn't talk to her for days. She would point to the things she wanted done and flick her fingers. Kimi had been punished this way before. It hurt more than harsh words.

Kimi blinked away unhappy memories and thought about the good ones—there were enough to fill the lake and still spill into the sea beyond. Kimi only had to look at Aunt Lu's small glances, the slight nods of approval, the brief pats on the hand. Aunt Lu bound her love tightly to her, a richer love in its quiet giving.

Heavy with the strong flavor of anise and ginger, the last bite of the dumpling lingered. Kimi pressed her finger into the crumbs sprinkled on the table in front of her, licking them off with the tip of her tongue.

When Aunt Lu finished her preparations, she lowered herself into a chair. Nearly as old as her brother, age had been kinder to her, leaving her with few wrinkles beyond those around her eyes and mouth. But her joints constantly ached, so Kimi had taken over the heavy chores.

Now it was Kimi's turn to tell what she'd learned in the town.

"What is it that you haven't told me yet?" Aunt Lu asked. "You tease me with the news. You will keep me up all night waiting for the end."

True. Kimi dragged out the telling and always saved the best for the end, but only because Aunt Lu preferred it that way, despite her complaints. Whenever Kimi tried to deliver the town's news in an efficient, orderly manner, her aunt's face would fall, making Kimi feel guilty. She waited while Aunt Lu poured herself a cup of tea.

"If you are tired, Aunt, I can tell you the rest in the morning."

"No, no. I'm sure whatever it is, I better hear it tonight. *Pah!* Tomorrow, with Xiao's visit, we will be too busy."

"Well, if you insist, then I must tell you. Mrs. Xie and several other women say they saw a black crane this morning."

Aunt Lu's eyes grew large and round. Her mouth dropped open, the heavy, porcelain cup she held toppled over, spilling the tea. Her fingers waved in a come-to-me motion, and Kimi gave her all the details—the words, the facial expressions, the muttered comments of those watching.

She left out Mei's goading. Aunt Lu would only say, "Ignore Mei. She isn't worthy of your notice. You have a special destiny."

Destiny or not, the taunting hurt.

Aunt Lu's mouth eventually closed and her eyes changed from round with surprise to narrow with worry.

"I knew it. Didn't I tell you about my dream? This is terrible, just terrible." She rubbed her temples. "We must be prepared."

Kimi had never seen her aunt so anxious—all because of a dream that probably meant nothing. "What will we prepare for?"

Aunt Lu looked at Kimi sharply with lips pressed thin and nostrils flaring. Why had her question made her aunt angry? It was reasonable enough.

"Anything. Everything. Flood. Famine. Fire. War. Cataclysm. To ignore the signs is to dig your own grave, girl."

Her aunt leaned forward, tension showing in her neck and shoulders. She was drawing fearsome conclusions from flimsy information.

"Perhaps it wasn't a black crane," Kimi said. "Maybe it was a flock of ordinary cranes against a dark cloud."

"Yes, and maybe a camel looks like a cat. The sky is perfectly clear. There have been no clouds for two days." Aunt Lu waggled her finger at her. "You listen too much to my brother. Not everything has a rational explanation. Some things just are. The gods don't have time to bother convincing those who won't believe. When you find your destiny, you will know."

Kimi held back a sigh. Destiny. Dragons. Gods. There were no gods. These superstitions were the women's way of dealing with unsettling news. That way if something bad happened, they could blame it on the gods. She would raise her daughters differently.

"But Zhi was with Mrs. Xie and she didn't see anything," she said, trying to bring her aunt back to her normal, sensible self.

"Zhi," her aunt said with derision. "What does she know? She can't see past the end of her nose. If Xie says there was a black crane, then there was a black crane. Remember, I told you about my dream? The gods are talking to us, and we'd better listen."

The only thing Kimi knew for sure was that both Mrs. Xie and Zhi were in the middle of the group of women talking about the dragon. Mrs. Xie's crane might be real. Maybe there were black cranes somewhere in China, and one got lost. But that didn't mean the gods sent it as a warning.

She hesitated before telling the rest of the women's gossip. If the black crane had her aunt so upset, how would she react to Lanfen's claim to have seen a dragon?

"Lanfen says she saw a dragon. And someone, I don't know who, said she dreamed of Empress Cixi's funeral. She said the god, Shang Ti, sent his chariot pulled by four phoenixes to carry the empress's coffin."

Aunt Lu looked at Kimi sharply. "A dragon? Are you sure? It's been a long time since anyone has seen a dragon. And with the cranes?" Aunt Lu pinched the bridge of her nose and winced. "It is too much. Trouble. Big trouble. And soon. Both sightings on the same day. There's no time, Kimi. No time at all."

"Lanfen said it was a dragon, but couldn't she mistake a crane for a dragon?"

Her aunt tilted her head as if to repeat her comment about a cat and a camel. "Perhaps. But maybe she really did see one. Once China had many dragons."

Not likely. Kimi pressed the last of the crumbs with her thumb.

"You doubt, girl. But someday you will see something you can't explain with logic, then you'll believe, Tengshe, you who soars." Her aunt's intense glare made Kimi squirm, but Aunt Lu wasn't done.

"You believe in tigers, don't you? Yet you haven't seen one. So why not dragons? Why would both a dragon and a tiger be set at the door of every temple to protect us if only the tiger were real?"

Kimi lowered her head. To protect us from evil spirits? As though an angry spirit, if there were such a thing, would be afraid of a stone statue. According to Aunt Lu, the only thing that would make a demon go away was resolution of the vengeance that sent the spirit walking in the first place.

"Humph," her aunt muttered, signaling the end of the subject, at least for the moment.

Aunt Lu tapped her finger on the table, something she did when she was concentrating. Then she nodded to herself. "Yes, we will begin tomorrow. I will order supplies. We will clean out the closets and shed to make room. The next day…"

Her aunt began listing chores and things to buy. It would be Kimi's job to do most of the work. Someone else did the bending, lifting, and carrying in Mei's house. If she were lucky, Kimi would have servants someday so she could have time to study and to teach.

The men's voices from the back of the house rose and fell, one high and old, the other low and full of life. This was the family Kimi knew. Aunt Lu fussed. Grandfather taught even now, and Xiao still argued with him. For a brief moment there were no Japanese on the doorstep, no Mei digging barbs deep into her flesh, no uncertainty about her future. At that moment everything was the way it should be.

Chapter Three

As Shi-lin traveled through China, she favored the Province of Manchuria, particularly the city of Pianshan.

Birds, bright sparks of a dozen hues, winged through the forests nearby, gliding through the brisk winds of spring and fall. She followed the cranes to their nesting grounds and the tigers into their mountain lairs. She loved the pristine whiteness of the snow and the drowsy warmth of the summer.

Veiled by magic, she often followed those who intrigued her, wanting to know the small details of their lives. A young man named Tuan captured her interest most of all. Each month he traveled to the city to sell the beautiful chests he made. Of all the things she found in the market, his exquisite work delighted her most. The carvings captured the splendor of the mountains and richness of the valleys.

* * *

"Hurry up!" Aunt Lu shouted from the back of the house.

Kimi sat in a bright square of morning sunlight on the floor of the hallway, piles of folded fabric on both sides and a small storage box in front of her. With one hand resting on the top of the closest pile, she sighed and closed her eyes. The choices were too hard. Still, she had to keep the salmon colored silk with the green bamboo embroidery. It made her skin look rosy, and she loved the way it cascaded over her hand when she held it—smooth as a waterfall. Aunt Lu's orders had been firm: one box only. Aunt Lu wanted the closets cleaned out as quickly as possible because the disaster could come on them any minute, so she needed space for blankets, rice, and extra warm clothing. Only the most precious possessions would be kept.

What if Kimi hid her favorites somewhere safe?

"You are a foolish girl," her aunt said, arriving from the back of the house to stand over Kimi's shoulder. "If you marry a rich man, you can buy all the silk you can wear. If you marry a poor man, what use will fancy clothes be? And if we don't survive the disaster that's coming, embroideries won't matter at all."

Even though Aunt Lu was behind Kimi's back, Kimi knew that her aunt stood with her hands on her hips and an impatient scowl on her face. Kimi loved her, but Aunt Lu could be annoying when in one of her moods.

"Make your choices and fill the trunk, or I will fill it for you. There's more to be done."

Kimi closed her eyes and touched her medallion for patience. Always more to be done.

The sound of footsteps coming from the direction of the back door interrupted her thoughts. Xiao.

"Go talk to Xiao," Aunt Lu said. "Ask him how your grandfather seemed - if he's seen a decline."

Kimi met Xiao in the hall. His face showed no emotion. She felt clumsy facing him with her hair a mess from packing. The thought peeved her. Why should she care what he thought?

Xiao's face was fixed in a polite mask. Tension grabbed hold of Kimi again. Lesser scholars and functionaries were probably intimidated by the mere power of his being. She refused to be impressed by a boy she'd played with as a child.

Kimi straightened her shoulders and asked, "How was grandfather when you left?"

"Perhaps a bit tired, but he did not appear to be in much pain."

"That is good."

"And how have you been, Kimi? Are you keeping yourself busy with suitors?" His eyes danced to match the smile on his lips.

He was treating her like a child. He might have been Grandfather's favorite student, and her best friend, but that didn't mean he could return and manage her life. She thought better of it before snapping out a sharp reply.

"No. I have more important things to do than worry about finding a husband."

Xiao let out a deep breath. "Your grandfather and Aunt Lu are old. I would think you'd want to marry. To have a family of your own. But never marry someone you don't love. Love is important."

It seemed he knew about love. Perhaps was in love. And that thought pinched. Why would she care if he had a dozen lovers? "Do you have someone you wish to marry?" Kimi asked.

"Not yet." He pushed away from the wall, still smiling his maddening smile. "I think I will walk by the lake and watch the cranes. It is possible that I will see the black one. And, who knows, maybe a dragon."

"You never know what you'll see," Kimi said. Her sarcasm merged into worry. "Maybe you will see the Japanese army marching toward Kaisun."

"I will watch." His face was serious as he left.

* * *

"You aren't paying attention to me," Mei huffed. "Didn't you hear?"

Kimi wound her way between agitated shoppers with Mei one step behind. A dozen women and even some men crowded around the carts at the center of the square shouting out prices.

"Did somebody die?" Kimi asked.

"I knew you weren't listening. It's Lushan."

Kimi shaded her eyes from the bright morning sun and studied the frantic activity in the market. Men stood in tight clusters at the fringe of the crowd looking worriedly over their shoulders. Women pushed and jostled around the farmer's carts in the middle of the square, buying everything in sight, loading handcarts instead of baskets. She wondered if there had been another "dragon" sighting.

"What about Lushan?" Kimi asked, pulling her attention away from the crowd.

"It's been invaded! The Japanese have taken Lushan! Some say they killed everyone."

Kimi stopped and turned, bumping in to someone's overfull basket.

"Watch where you're going!" the owner of the basket snapped, glaring at Kimi.

This couldn't be true. It wasn't possible that they had killed thirty thousand people. How big was their army? Kimi's spine tingled and her body flushed with warmth. She grabbed Mei's arm and dragged her closer to the apothecary's shop where it was less crowded. "Who told you Lushan has been invaded?"

"The baker's brother-in-law delivered a telegram to my father a little over an hour ago."

Dread settled into Kimi's stomach. "Who sent it? What did it say?"

Mei threw up her hands. "Somebody in Lushan. Maybe a clerk. I don't know. Does it matter?"

"Of course it matters." How could he send a message if everyone was dead? Had he died after sending the message?

"Well, my father believes it," Mei said. "He telegraphed the empress, asking for more soldiers. Only as a precaution. He said Kaisun isn't in any danger."

If true, why were Mei's family servants among those crowding the carts with baskets overflowing? Kimi sensed that Mei's bragging thinly covered the fear leaking around the edges of her confident mask.

Several businessmen sidestepped a full cart. They bumped up against Kimi and Mei, bringing their animated conversation with them.

"Will they come this far north?" Raggu, the tailor, asked. He and his wife expected their first baby any day.

"Why would they bother with Kaisun?" Raggu's brother asked.

"Why would they bother with Korea? Most of Korea's villages are no bigger than ours. Still, the Japanese march on Korea every few years." Despite his confident words, Raggu's brother pulled his overfull cart closer to his side.

"*Pah!* Japan can't expect to invade China. They are so much smaller—a flea biting a dog," the tailor said. "It's only Lushan they want."

Raggu's brother stopped and looked at his brother. "That, and all the other ports on the Yellow Sea. Pirates, that's what they are."

"We shouldn't trust Japan," the tailor said.

Kimi agreed with this.

Widow Shikai elbowed her way through the men to where Kimi and Mei stood. "Are you in line?" Shikai asked.

"No," Mei replied.

Kimi hadn't noticed a line forming outside the apothecary's shop. If Lushan really had been taken, Kimi wanted to buy Grandfather's medicine while the apothecary still had the ingredients.

"Yes," Kimi corrected, moving into position.

Mei took a step back. "I don't want to wait for your grandfather's medicine. Besides, I need to help my mother."

Mei merged back into the crowd to where several carts had joined the throng of women and their baskets at the center of the market. On the fringe of the crowd not far from Kimi, an old woman stood, watching the commotion. Kimi didn't remember seeing her before. Perhaps she was someone's grandmother who came to live here. She wore her worn clothes in an elegant, upright, almost regal way. Her faded and frayed blue silk jacket was embroidered with cranes. The skirt was simple brown cotton.

Kimi looked to see if anyone was nearby acting as escort. No one. The old woman was alone. When Kimi turned back to look at the old woman again, she wasn't there. She scanned the crowd but saw no sign of her. Odd, but Kimi dismissed it.

The commotion in the market increased. Were these people foolish, fleeing before an enemy was in sight? In the midst of the chaos, Mister Cho, the baker, stood planted on the stone road in front of his shop like a tree in a flood. He swept the road and shook his head at no one in particular. Japanese soldiers would have to grab his broom before he would accept the truth of what others said.

Should she make Aunt Lu and Grandfather leave and look for a safe place to hide? Just in case? Would Aunt Lu expect Kimi's 'destiny' to protect them somehow?

The urge to hurry home grew. Once finished at the apothecary's, Kimi rushed to the road, carrying a double order of her grandfather's medicine. Already families were trudging by with their life's possessions loaded on carts or strapped to their backs.

Worry made her breath come shallow and fast. She forced herself to take deep breaths as she followed the cart tracks down the hill. Why would the Japanese come to Kaisun? It didn't make any sense. They would cross to Peking if they had the strength, or perhaps go up the Liao River to the Summer Palace, trapping the Empress if she was still there. Dividing their forces seemed foolish. She took another deep, ragged breath. She had been caught up in the frenzy. That was all. She would feel foolish when this was all over.

Making her way down the hill, Kimi began to feel faint. She stepped aside from the departing villagers to catch her breath.

How the gold and red leaves had deepened overnight so that they glowed in the afternoon sun, how the air smelled sharp and clean, and how the lake sparkled in amber drops as little wavelets rippled across the surface, lapping at the shore on the side of the road. A flock of cranes glided overhead; their long necks and snowy bodies stretched toward their winter homes. No black one, though.

Chapter Four

Like Shi-lin, Tuan was a solitary person, remaining apart from his fellows, speaking only to those who came to buy his chests. He watched the people who passed with interest and smiled quietly to himself.

Shi-lin followed him to his small house near the monastery on the Mountain of the Morning Song. Hidden by her magic, she watched him make his chests. He carved the sides and top, then painstakingly formed the joints so well they could not be seen. She stood by, less than a shadow, as he tended his fields in the afternoon. And in the evening, she would sit as he played a wooden flute, entranced by the mellow sounds of his music.

* * *

The villagers were panicking for no good reason, but the feeling of calm Kimi had built around herself gave way. She ran the rest of the way home with her lungs on fire. Despite the chill breeze, perspiration dotted her forehead when she arrived. She stood in the hallway for a moment to catch her breath. Stacks of emergency supplies piled in the corner of the entry waited to be moved into the closets she was emptying.

She gave a nod to the tiger painted onto the three silk panels over the table. When she was little she had been afraid of it, convinced it could walk off the panels in the dark. Now she acknowledged it with a nod as she passed. Silly, but it made her feel better.

"Is that you, Kimi?" Aunt Lu called.

"Coming," she said, setting the package of medicine on the narrow table under the tiger.

Aunt Lu, surrounded by a mound of radishes, peeled one into a ceramic bowl. The bowl was painted with symbols of the four dragons—black, red, blue, and green—that guarded the seas and rivers of China.

Dragons. The women and their superstitions. Dragons had surrounded Kimi her whole life.

Aunt Lu lifted her knife and waved it in the direction of Kimi's chair. "You are back early."

"Aunt Lu, I must speak with Grandfather. If Xiao is with him, I'm sure he'll want to know as well. You will, too."

Aunt Lu shook her head. "Xiao left this morning, shortly after you did."

"Already? I know you said his stay would be short, but this short?"

"He didn't say where he was going, only that he would be back this afternoon. He seemed rather in a rush. But he will leave after he says goodbye."

She gave Kimi a probing look. "As for my brother... If he is napping, you let him be. Your news can wait until later."

"The Japanese control Lushan," Kimi blurted.

Aunt Lu pressed her lips tight and waggled the hand holding the knife. "You see, girl, I told you something terrible would happen. I dreamed about the black crane again." She shook her head, going back to chopping radishes at double speed.

"Now, don't fret child. This has happened before. You remember the violence last year when the Righteous and Harmonious Fist threatened to rid China of all Foreign Devils? Before that it was the Taiping Rebellion, but you were too young to remember. And before that the White Lotus. And before that... Still, here we are. Kaisun is a long way from Lushan. Our food and supplies may be delayed while their army takes first pick. An army is like a horde of thieving locusts."

She tapped her temple with her finger. "I am smart. The gods warned me. You wait and see. We will have enough. They will take everything they want from Lushan and go on to Peking and be stopped by the Empress's soldiers."

Aunt Lu picked up another long, white radish. "It's the port they want. Now they have it. There's no rush. Let your grandfather sleep."

"Can I at least see if he's awake?"

Aunt Lu huffed and nodded.

Kimi tiptoed to Grandfather's door, peering in to see if he slept. He was propped against the dragon carved into the mahogany headboard, reading.

He raised his head. The thin line of his mouth turned up, a faint memory of the full smile that had once filled his face. Kimi wished she could find a magic flower to remove the pain and make him well. But magic didn't exist, and it broke her heart to watch him dwindle. She hesitated to add the burden of her news.

He set the book on the table, pushing the bottle of medicine out of the way.

"So grim. What worries you, child?"

Kimi sat on the side of the bed, folding her hands in her lap. "The Japanese have taken Lushan. No one survived."

He stroked his chin and gave his head a small shake. "Someone surely survived to send out word. When did this happen?" His tone was calm—curious, but calm.

She leaned forward. "The Japanese were there yesterday. Mei said Cho's brother-in-law delivered a telegram to Mei's father not three hours ago. People are leaving. They say the Japanese are coming."

He plucked at the embroidery on the bedspread. "This is indeed unfortunate news. For years the Empress contended with the Europeans who still want access to our ports. The Russians want to build their railroad through Manchuria. And now the Japanese intrude. The Europeans and Russians will not support Japan's effrontery. This will not end well for Japan."

"Kimi, this morning Xiao told me the Japanese have taken Dandong. They crossed the Yalu River from Korea in the middle of the night over an impossible bridge made of pontoons. Such a feat would inspire awe if our soldiers accomplished it. In these circumstances, it inspires fear. Xiao said that Dandong fell easily. Surrounded by mountains on three sides and the river on the fourth, they felt safe."

"How did Xiao know this, Grandfather? How long ago did it happen?"

"I believe it happened yesterday. I don't know how Xiao knew. The Empress has a chain of messengers throughout China. Perhaps one contacted him last night."

Kimi clenched her hands. "Didn't the people of Dandong fight to cut off the bridge?"

"In the middle of the night? And who would fight the invaders? The Empress's soldiers in Dandong, if there were any, were probably sleeping off too much wine." He shook his head. His mouth pursed, making him look as though he had bitten into a green plum. "Xiao says that people woke to see Japanese soldiers in the street. Not much bloodshed."

He rubbed the side of his nose. "So, now they have taken Lushan as well."

Fear gripped Kimi firmly in its claws. What about the god-ordained destiny Aunt Lu talked about? What good is trying to build a school when the Japanese are attacking us? Her dreams for her future seemed to fade into darkness.

The fearful claw that held Kimi tightened. "Where will they go next?"

Grandfather switched from plucking the bedspread to tracing the pattern of the design, something he did when deep in thought. "The Japanese navy will ensure they hold Lushan, then they'll go to the port at Tenggu and follow the road to Peking. At least that is where I would go if I had an army sufficiently large to suppress Lushan so quickly." He drew his fingers to a steeple and touched them to his lips.

"Grandfather, we should go. There is a safe place in the woods, the old woodshed Xiao and I played in. I bought extra medicine. We can pack as many supplies as we can carry, and maybe I can come back for more."

"You get ahead of yourself. It is doubtful they will come at all, and certainly there will be warning. Even so, I will not leave my home. It is you who must go."

Grandfather closed his eyes for a moment. Kimi examined his sunken cheeks, took in his trembling hands. She knew the truth. He lacked the strength to leave, not the courage. She would remain with them. "If you stay, I stay. I won't abandon you or Aunt Lu. You are my family."

He shook his head. A tiny flare of strength returned. "It is a problem we do not need to solve. The Japanese will not come here."

"But what of Xiao? I assume he's going back to Peking. What if he's on the road all alone when the Japanese arrive?" A tic fluttered at Kimi's temple. "And the troops who took Dandong? Won't they come south to join those at Lushan?" Kimi inched forward on her chair. "Do you think they will try to capture all of Manchuria?"

Grandfather reached across and patted her hands. His dry, papery skin was soft. A mild tremble had settled into his bones and his pulse beat as shallow and fast as a dove's. Many times she had watched him sleep, knowing there would come a day when he wouldn't wake.

"Do not worry," he said. "Xiao will be safe. The Forbidden City is a fortress. The Empress may have ignored her provinces, but she has not ignored the capitol or the Summer Palace. I have watched the Japanese for decades. They are not foolish. The soldiers at Dandong will go directly west toward the Summer Palace. The ones at Lushan to Peking. Rest assured, China has never fallen. It never will."

He nodded. So much sadness in his eyes. He never talked about the past much.

He paused and the worry faded from his face. "We will consider these things later when there is more information."

Kimi saw the tired lines on Grandfather's face and turned to go. "You need your rest. We will talk later."

"Kimi." The way he said her name made her pause.

"Yes, Grandfather."

"Xiao and I talked of you. My sister is old, and I have little time left. Xiao is a good man. An important man. I promised you to him in marriage. It is a good match. Knowing the two of you will be together brings me peace."

It would take time to absorb this news. When Kimi found her voice, she said, "Yes, Grandfather."

"Xiao will not force you to honor my promise. It will be your choice."

The tension in Kimi eased its stronghold. She couldn't hold back her smile as she walked toward the kitchen.

After a long while, Kimi's mind left thoughts of marriage and returned to the Japanese. A feather of panic remained. When would they have more information? When the Japanese were marching through Kaisun?

If Grandfather refused to go, Kimi would find a way to make him even if she had to carry him on her back. She had lost her mother; she would not lose Grandfather.

Chapter Five

By the time the peonies bloomed, Shi-lin began to visit the market in the shape of a young woman so she could speak with Tuan. She asked him all the questions that had been burning on her tongue, most especially about the stories and places he portrayed in his carvings. Each month he added to her store of knowledge. Though she reveled in their discussions, she knew a time would come when her need to be a dragon and his need to be human would drive them apart.

Late one day, after Tuan had readied his cart for his journey home, he sat beside Shi-lin, but said nothing. He watched an ant carry a breadcrumb across a cobblestone. He looked at Shi-lin out of the corner of his eye. Shi-lin wondered what troubled him so much that he could not speak of it directly.

"Shi-lin, tell me of your family. Do you have many brothers? Is your father well?"

This question surprised Shi-lin. She wondered why he had not asked this before, grateful she'd avoided the troublesome topic until now. But it was a troublesome topic and she did not know what to tell him. She hoped that by diverting his question she could avoid divulging the truth of her heritage.

"I do not know my father well. My mother is kindly. Please tell me of your family. Surely they are more interesting."

He told her of his father, of his three brothers, and of the life he had made for himself. He described his home in such loving detail it transported her. But she already knew its beauty, for she had followed him there often and had seen it in all its seasons—the green seas of forest, the majesty of his mountains, and the lake near his house where she could watch deer come to water themselves in the evening.

Month after month Shi-lin followed him into the city. Shi-lin knew that her growing interest in Tuan was improper. She fought her urges, attempting to stay away from his mountain home. But no amount of self-restraint could keep her from meeting him in the market each month.

Over time, their conversations became longer, then longer still as the summer ripened their friendship. She loved to sit with him as he waited for buyers.

She found it increasingly difficult to remain hidden when she followed him to his home in the mountains, particularly in the evenings when the joy of his music echoed with loneliness and he stared wistfully out his window. She wanted to ask him what he saw and why he seemed so sorrowful.

* * *

When the summer flowers began to drop their seeds, Shi-lin's time with Tuan in the market grew into long periods of contented silence. She caught his shy glances when he thought she was not looking and understood that he, too, wanted their brief visits to never end. When she followed him to his home, she heard longing in the song of his flute and longing in the silence when he didn't play.

Tuan lingered in the market one day after his last chest had been sold. He spoke with Shi-lin of inconsequential things as they sometimes did. But Shi-lin knew that something troubled him. For the first time their conversation stuttered, ending in a long, uncomfortable silence.

He turned to her at last, his brow furrowed and tense. "Shi-lin. You have told me little of your family. You say that your father is a traveler, but I would speak with him, if I may. Please tell me how I may reach him."

Shi-lin's heart ached. She had both longed for and dreaded this moment.

"That is not possible," she replied. Her father, the great dragon king, would laugh and dismiss Tuan without a moment's thought.

"Is there no one I can speak with? I wish to ask if we might wed." He looked to her, and she could see how much he desired this union and how fearful he was that she would not agree.

She could not ease his mind. "I have treasured our time together and have hoped that our friendship would continue, but this one wish I may not be able to grant."

She saw pain on his face and regretted that she had been the one to put it there. "I will consider your offer and speak with my mother. When we meet again in a month, I will tell you my answer."

* * *

Kimi leaned back, bracing her arms on the stone bench at the side of the small garden pool, letting the afternoon sun bathe her face.

Cleaning the shed was a punishing task. Humans had ignored it for years. Too bad the mice, spiders, and moths hadn't ignored it as well. She shuddered and then reached up to remove her scarf, touching only the edges in case there was living cargo. She shook the scarf, folded it, and used the clean side to wipe perspiration from her temples. At least she had been left to do the job her own way.

"Make the storage shed ready," Aunt Lu had said. Piles of emergency supplies were stacked in the entry, waiting to be brought out to the shed. All this work and the Japanese probably wouldn't even come to Kaisun.

For now it felt good to sit and listen as water dribbled from the streamlet into the pool where the carp swam. For a moment she could rest her worries about the Japanese. Instead, she recalled childhood memories of the mellow tones of Xiao's flute when he thought no one listened. She could feel his soul soar on the threads of music.

Kimi's heart soared beside those remembered threads. She was going to marry Xiao. Not a pig farmer. Not an old sailor. Not even a merchant who scrabbled for a living in the markets. Grandfather said Xiao loved her—had always loved her. She swung her feet, feeling the sun's warmth all the way to her bones. She imagined lying in his arms. The heat spread to her cheeks.

Still, a thought nagged. Would he understand her desire to help others like her—foundlings, girls who sought to learn? They'd been such good friends. Surely he would want her happiness.

A frog crouched on a rock between the draping branches of a creeping cedar. Brown tinged the edges of the purple water irises that rose from the shallow pond. With the first hard frost they would be gone. She looked up at branches of the maple making a temple arch over the pond. So far, only a few leaves had fallen. Soon they would come like golden snowfall, and she would rake them up each day, leaving them in a large mound outside the back gate of the garden.

She took a deep breath of air—crisp and tingled with hints of pine needles, maple leaves, and dew. Would Xiao's home have a garden? For sure. He needed the serenity as much as she did.

Xiao arrived so quietly that her heart jumped when he sat beside her. She brushed thick dust from the front of her trousers. He studied her for a moment, then looked out over the garden. Kimi looked at her dusty shoes. "Aunt Lu wants me to clean the storeroom."

"It must be very hot work."

She glanced at him from the side. He must know that Grandfather had spoken to her. She tucked her hands under her legs, not sure what to do with them.

The ginger cat leapt onto the bench between them, leaned into Xiao's arm, and purred. Xiao scratched the cat behind the ears. "Your aunt told me about the black crane. Do you think it has come as a warning?"

Kimi almost laughed out loud. While she had lain awake last night, she had tried to imagine all of the things he would say to her. Cranes were not on the list.

A small smile escaped. "I don't think we need a portent to tell us that this is a time of change. Superstitions and legends won't help with the Westerners or the Japanese."

She caught herself lecturing and stopped. Maybe she was a touch nervous. Maybe he was nervous, too. She watched his face.

Xiao sat rigidly with one hand on his thigh, the other on the cat's back. Very formal—except for the cat. He stared at the clouds. Not at all like the old Xiao. He had always been so full of questions, so eager. He raced through his days. Aunt Lu repeatedly scolded him at mealtimes, insisting he slow down and not talk so much.

Now he spoke, directing his words into the distance. "It may be that some of the legends are true. We need the myths. China needs its dragons." He turned to her, looking like he meant it and wanted her to agree.

How preposterous! He sounded like Aunt Lu.

Kimi couldn't keep her frustration out of her voice. "China needs to be freed of the bindings that hold it in the past."

Now his eyes shone with passion; he lifted his hands, imploring. "Without those bindings, China will become another machine like Britain, Germany, and America. Like them we will march unbridled into the future, embracing progress without measuring the cost."

With Xiao's movement, the ginger cat stepped over to Kimi's lap and kneaded her thighs, its claws prickling her skin. She lifted the cat and set it on the other side of the bench.

Xiao kept his gaze on the cat instead of Kimi. In a quieter voice he continued, "All people need mystery. People who allow only what science and reason teach live half-lives. They never reach into the part of themselves that can be amazed, can feel wonder, can touch beauty." He looked at Kimi, his eyes nearly begging. "Kimi, the legends give us power far greater than anything we can manage on our own."

He had the calm assurance of a born leader. People would follow him. But, according to him, she was one of those people who lived a half-life.

Her back stiffened. "Science can create just as much wonder."

He smiled in a way that reminded her of Grandfather. "If we lose the legends, we lose ourselves. China will have no heart left if the legends die."

Kimi's jaw clenched. He was lecturing her. She leaned forward, making sure she had his attention completely. "Perhaps people have lived too long with the expectation that magic and god-sent miracles will solve all their problems. Maybe that is why China hasn't changed."

A gentle smile tugged at his mouth.

How could Xiao think this way? Grandfather didn't raise us to believe in the old women's tales. Where did this belief in magic come from?

Xiao shrugged. "Your grandfather never denied the legends. Did you ever ask him? I assure you, he never would have said such a thing."

"Grandfather never denied the existence of spirits, even spirits perverted by vengeful grief. But he never agreed that magic existed or that legendary creatures, or even gods are real."

Kimi bit her lip to keep from saying anything she would regret. As children they had debated for hours, playfully, holding their positions until one of them admitted defeat. But this didn't feel like their old bantering. What a stupid topic to argue about. He was certain he was right and she was sure he was wrong. She wished for a moment that Grandfather would resolve the debate, but they weren't children anymore.

"Why has China stayed locked inside itself?" she asked.

Xiao held up his hands like a wall between them. "Don't blame the dragons. China is old. The weight of history bears us down. From time to time, someone with new ideas steps forward. People rebel, new dynasties begin, but the rebellions are crushed, the emperors issue decrees, and China goes on the way it always has."

How did this turn into a debate about dragons? She didn't want to argue like this after they married—not about the existence of dragons or magic or other legends or anything else.

She stared at the pond. He had been her friend; he would be her friend again. After all, this was just a silly debate.

The silence stretched.

A frog sunning itself on the rocks plopped into the pond. The sound of its splash startled Kimi. The weight of the broken silence settled over her. Time for a new subject. "What will the ministers in Peking do about Japan's invasion at Lushan? They will send the army, won't they?"

His face remained calm, but his eyes flashed fiercely, causing her to pull back a little. Clearly, she'd asked the wrong question.

"Do? The Empress will argue with her ministers and do nothing. The ministers will expect Manchuria to manage its own problems." His gaze left her face and returned to the garden. His bitter words weren't directed at her. This time she felt tension in his stillness. His anger radiated as though he were a furnace.

There had to be a story hidden in those angry words.

She waited, hoping he would explain.

When he looked up at her again, the fierceness was gone. Instead, he looked at her with his eyes open wide as though her face held the answer to a question he hadn't asked. She briefly felt herself fall into that odd mood again where she imagined his every twitch and word would change the roots of the earth.

He brought his hands together and rubbed them, palm against palm. "I have left the Empress's Court." Soft words said as plain fact.

She gripped his arm then pulled her hand back. "Why?"

She couldn't believe what she had heard. People devoted their lives seeking a place at court, and he'd walked away?

The cat settled between them again, keeping a paw on Kimi's thigh. She scratched the cat's ears while Xiao, apparently without thought, rubbed his hands down the cat's back, narrowly missing her fingers. She felt a spark bridge the gap between their fingers and drew her fingers back, hoping he wouldn't notice how shaky he made her feel.

"I am not suited for that life." He made the statement without inflection, as if commenting on the rice crop.

Kimi's hands clutched the edge of the bench. "Why aren't you suited? It's what you always wanted. What happened?"

"Nothing happened. That is what went wrong."

She could see how his fingers blanched where they curved around the stone bench.

His words were tinged with resentment. "Although I wished to aid the voices of reason, I was deflected. Some ministers plotted devious ways to get the Empress's notice while others plotted ways to rebel against her. I met few men of integrity, and those had little or no influence. The Empress surrounds herself with men she can manipulate. Men who will tell her exactly what she wishes to hear."

Kimi winced. It would be awful to have studied so hard and have no one listen. But if he were cautious, he would eventually be able to influence the Court. He was a leader. She had heard that in his voice. Why give up now? Surely there must be another way.

"So, what will you do now?"

His eyes seemed to bore his frustration into her mind. "No, nobody dismissed me. I tired of the dance and left. I have a home in the mountains. I will plant potatoes." He said it evenly, as though such a statement made all the sense in the world.

Her hands fell limp in her lap. "Potatoes?" She could hear Mei saying, "I'll bet your grandfather will find you a desperate, old pig farmer to marry."

Her mind filled with images of a timber and clay hovel perched on the edge of a rocky hill, miles from neighbors. She imagined pigs and geese wandering the yard. She could smell the wood smoke and feel the biting cold of the mountain air. The thought of bathing in icy water made goose bumps on her arms. She felt despair fall like coils of creeper vine binding her. And each image that came into her head tightened the coils until she struggled to breathe.

Was this the destiny her mother's note promised—the destiny that had its hand on her soul? Farmwife? She could almost feel the mahjong tiles fall as the wall broke in front of her. She loved Xiao, at least she thought she did, but she had hoped their marriage would also help her fulfill her lifelong dreams. All night she had thought about the things she could do while he attended to the Empress's business.

Tendrils of righteous anger grew. Xiao had planned her future without including her in the discussion. Had he even told Grandfather?

She stood, clenched her fists. "What about my plans? And yours? What happened to the joyous future you envisioned when we were children? You studied all those years so you could plant potatoes? You expect me to live on a farm and plant potatoes with you?"

His face went chalk white. He stood, his tall frame bent so that their noses were inches apart. "Yes, I hoped you would."

"Leave the court if you must, but find a position that makes more sense. Teach at one of the new universities. Become magistrate of a town. Improve things. Do something to make a difference."

"I can do as much good for China from the mountains as I can from any city."

"I don't see how."

They stared at each other for several minutes, but she wouldn't weaken her argument with an apology.

He started to speak but stopped. He stayed so still he looked like a statue of white jade and onyx.

She sat, her eyes unfocused as her mind spun and swirled. She didn't see a way out of this. Moisture gathered in her eyes. She bit her lip to keep tears from falling. Surely he had anticipated how unhappy this news would make her.

His eyes implored her and his hand reached out.

Kimi wanted to take his hand and bridge the rift between them, but her heart was too stung. Was he really the man she thought she knew? Dragons? Potatoes? Her fingers curled so that her nails bit her palms.

"I won't ask you to marry against your will. I must leave this afternoon to finish some business in Peking. But I will return in the spring. If your heart remains fixed against sharing the life of a potato farmer, I will release you from your grandfather's promise."

His footsteps made no sound as he walked away.

* * *

When Kimi went to bed that night she found a small lacquered box on her pillow with a note underneath.

"I did not mean to tell you in this way, but I do love you, Tengshe."

Beating dreadfully, her heart echoed the pain she felt as she opened her hand to lift the shiny black box. A dragon inlay, made of rippling blue shades of nacre, decorated the top. Sadness filled her. Dragons. Legends. Myths.

She removed the tiny pin that kept the lid shut. Letting it dangle from the fine chain that held the key to the box, she lifted the lid.

Chapter Six

Troubled in spirit at the unusual turning of her life, Shi-lin journeyed to her dragon home in the Yellow Sea. Amid the richness of the Dragon King's castle, she surrounded herself with the elements of her dragon life. She raced among the waves and flew high into the heavens. She sought the roots of her soul.

When she searched her heart, she found Tuan so tightly bound there that it would not beat without him.

* * *

"Kimi! Wake up, girl." Aunt Lu shook Kimi's shoulder. Kimi's heart raced when she realized something must be terribly wrong. Grandfather. Was he dying? Was he dead?

She opened her eyes and saw Aunt Lu leaning over her, a lantern held in one hand. The sooty smell of oil mingled with the wavering light.

"Grandfather?" She flung her legs over the bed, hardly noticing the biting chill. She grabbed the soft silk robe draped over the end of the bed, pushing an arm through a sleeve as she raced behind her aunt.

"He is fine. Follow me. Hurry, girl!" Her aunt's tone dismissed her concern, leaving Kimi puzzled. As she waited for an explanation, her Aunt Lu pushed her roughly into the hall.

Aunt Lu nudged Kimi into Grandfather's bedroom. Just inside the door Kimi stopped when she saw the disorder. She wrapped her arms around her waist. "What's wrong?"

Grandfather didn't look up. He stood at his dresser, pulling clothes out and tossing them onto the unmade bed. A half-full carry sack rested near the pillows. Had they finally decided to listen to her and go into hiding?

"Grandfather, what are you doing?" A frantic edge crept into Kimi's voice.

He nodded when he closed the drawer and turned to face her. Eyes shining with fever, wisps of hair formed a white halo around his head. "Come. We do not have much time."

No time for what? The clock beside his bed marked two hours before midnight.

He crossed the room to his desk, moving more quickly than she had seen in over a year. Kimi stretched her hands out to protect him from falling. But Aunt Lu pushed her toward the bed, pointing to the pile of Grandfather's clothes. "Put those things on." Muttering about hiding the rest of Kimi's things, she scurried out of the room.

"Grandfather, what's happened?"

"In a minute…"

Kimi grabbed the clothing and went to the paneled screen in the corner. She draped the clothes over the top of the rosewood screen. The screen where the carved crane forever waited among the reeds. The plain brown pants she pulled on were her grandfather's work pants, but he hadn't worn them for a year. She swallowed a painful lump, knowing he would never plant peonies again. She put her arms through the sleeves of his shirt, fastening the front and folding back the sleeves.

When she stepped from behind the screen she found her grandfather bending over a desk opening a small, flat box she had never seen before.

"Grandfather, please..." Her voice quavered.

He motioned for her to be still. Dozens of silver bars clinked together as he lifted them a fistful at a time from the box onto the silk panel—the last he had painted since his illness.

She gasped, her question forgotten. So much money. Why had they lived so frugally?

He spread the little bars evenly on the silk. His fingers worked quickly—folding, placing bars, and folding again so that the metal no longer touched metal.

As he tucked the money away, he spoke. "A runner came from the city a few minutes ago." His voice remained calm, but his movements were hurried, and deep worry lines crossed his brow. The unhealthy shine of his eyes belied his seeming calmness. "The boy said the Japanese are in the village. They are turning people out of their homes. He said there has been killing and worse."

What could be worse than killing? Certainly this was a hoax. She would wake up any minute from this dream. "You said they wouldn't come to Kaisun."

He massaged his temple. "I was wrong."

The edges of Kimi's world crashed. Grandfather was never wrong. He turned back to his task, but he wasn't the same. His confidence was gone. Her heart ached, wishing to go back in time. Even one day.

She stepped toward him, but he waved her away. "Finish dressing. There is not much time."

She put on his thick jacket that still lay on the bed, touching the edge of the pocket where she had mended a torn corner. She shivered, too confused to be afraid. "Why are you still in your night clothes? You should be changing, too."

"My sister and I are not coming. I am too old and too sick. If they think we are here alone, they will not search for you. Wear the socks. It will be cold."

No. This was wrong.

Kimi dropped into the chair beside Grandfather's bed, the socks dangling from her fingers. Thoughts darted like startled fish. She tried to think of another plan, some way to make him come with her, but her mind wouldn't settle long enough.

Grandfather shoved the wrapped money into the bottom of her pack. "Take this money, but do not let anyone see it." He handed her another pile of coins—ones of smaller denomination. "Put these in your pockets and shoes. If you make purchases, pay from the coins in your pocket. Others will see how little you have and not rob you."

Frustrated, she shook her head. "I won't need this." When she came back in the morning, the soldiers would be gone; all would be well.

"Grandfather, you can't do this. I won't let you. Either you come with me, or I will stay here until you decide to come, too."

He looked at her sharply. "You will do no such thing, child. I will not leave my home. You are strong but you cannot carry me as far as the storage shed or any other place you choose to hide."

Aunt Lu stomped in—imperious and angry. "*Pah!* I won't let you take my brother. Besides, if we are here the Japanese won't think to look for you."

"But if you are here, they will kill you." Grandfather sighed and looked far away for a moment. His eyes were sad when he faced her again. "If you are here, they will rape you and then kill you. I love you, daughter, I cannot let this happen."

Simmering, Kimi searched for another argument to convince him. None came.

"Quick, quick, girl!" Aunt Lu scolded, dropping the shoes at Kimi's feet before pushing a packet of food into the backpack. "Do not eat it all at once; it may be all you have for a while." Kimi heard the worry hiding behind the gruffness of those words. This had to be a bad dream. Grandfather seemed too calm, her aunt too frantic. Kimi couldn't put the puzzle pieces together.

The socks bunched uncomfortably when Kimi jammed her feet into the shoes. She tugged until some of the lumps smoothed out. When she looked up, Grandfather was blowing on a piece of paper. "These are directions to Xiao's home."

The unreal feeling hardened into sharp-edged fear. Certainly this wasn't necessary. Hiding was only a precaution.

Grandfather folded the paper into a small packet and put it in her outstretched hand. He closed her fingers over the note. Studying her, his eyes swam in a pool of tears. "Hide until the Japanese are gone."

He was saying goodbye. She felt answering tears come. Surely he was wrong. He patted her hand and stepped away.

"Honor requires I stay with you either here or in hiding," Kimi said.

Aunt Lu stepped over and shook Kimi's shoulder. "Honor requires that you follow my brother's instructions."

She was wrong. Caring for your elders was a much higher honor. Kimi would figure out a way to do both.

Grandfather closed the metal moneybox and slid it into a desk drawer. He turned to Kimi, concern stamped on his face. "Daughter, you must be careful. Don't return to the house. Leave Kaisun as quickly and as quietly as you can and go to Xiao. He will know what to do. The mountains are far, but you are strong."

"Xiao should be here. He left us to face this alone."

"I told him the Japanese would not come here. He trusted me. I am so sorry, Kimi. He is many miles west by now." Grandfather adjusted papers on his desk. "They will not capture Xiao. His long legs and youth will carry him faster than an army can move."

She wanted him to be right, but he had been wrong about the Japanese coming to Kaisun. "How can you be sure?"

Soft as a feather, he brushed stray hairs from her forehead. "The gods protect those they love. They will protect you too, child."

Kimi's chest tightened. There was so much to say to him, but the words remained locked inside. How he had been so much more than a father. How she treasured his lessons. How patient he was with all of her childish questions. But there wasn't time. When she touched his sleeve he pulled her against his chest. Kimi swallowed the lump in her throat when she realized she was probably saying goodbye forever. He released her, then turned and arranged the things on his desk, removing all signs of his hasty doings.

Aunt Lu turned Kimi toward her, pinning Kimi's arms, staring intently into her eyes. "Mind your grandfather. The Japanese will not be merciful. Gods will weep if you became a soldier's whore, if you even live that long. Go. Don't look back."

She would hide nearby, but not leave.

Aunt Lu released Kimi then turned to the pack on the bed. Now with a sash around the rolled-up blanket, Kimi slid her arms through, adjusting it so that it rested high on her back with the blanket at her waist. The pack didn't seem too heavy carried this way, just a bit clumsy.

Aunt Lu's awkward hug surprised her, even if it was only the briefest embrace. Aunt Lu wasn't affectionate in that way. Gripping Kimi's shoulders, Aunt Lu held her at arm's length, staring at Kimi's face as if trying to memorize it.

"Mind your grandfather, girl." Then she turned Kimi toward the door and pushed her forward. "Stay out of sight and leave no matter what you hear. Don't be foolish. May the ancestors protect you, child. Hurry!"

Kimi turned back for a moment and gathered in the sight of Grandfather leaning over his desk and Aunt Lu standing at the foot of his bed. These two people defined her world. So many times she'd seen him bend just so to add a stroke to a scroll. So many times he had stood to reach for a book. So many times he had adjusted the position of his ink stone to align it perfectly. And now he was putting away those symbols of his life. As always, his sister stood by—strong, capable, devoted completely to her brother. If Grandfather was the rock in Kimi's life, Aunt Lu was the water—bending, shaping, and forming. Kimi couldn't imagine life without them.

The glow of the lantern made shadows of their faces. Still, the glint of a tear on her aunt's face shimmered in the dim light, waiting to fall. Kimi did not have the strength to leave.

"Hurry, girl," Aunt Lu called behind her.

With one last look, Kimi turned away and walked out of Grandfather's room.

She found her way through the dark house and into the moon-washed garden. The long shadows of fence posts were prison bars locking the good within. Her heart thudded.

She leaned out just enough to see. What if the army was already in the road? For the moment the night was silent, as if holding its breath for what was to come.

Faint thumping came to her from a distance, just at the edge of hearing. Then pop! Pop! Followed by cruel laughter.

Kimi cringed. A sob rose in her throat, but she silenced it. She tried not to think about what the sounds might mean.

Several minutes of silence were interrupted by more thumping sounds. They were getting closer. If the Japanese hurt Grandfather or Aunt Lu, she vowed to hurt them and drive them from Manchuria one way or another.

A sharp crack. More laughter frayed her nerves. Guttural bursts, not the soft singing of the Chinese tongue.

She must drag Grandfather and Aunt Lu to the shed.

The sound of gunshots split the night air, followed by more laughter.

No time! No time! She turned back and fled the final distance to the garden shed.

Shutting the door behind her, Kimi moved to the back of the shed, repositioning the stack of boxes so that it looked like a solid wall.

The gate bell of the house next to hers clanked. Her heartbeat sounded nearly as loud.

She crouched into the safest place, the one she had intended as Grandfather's spot. The dragon medallion bumped cold beneath the shirt. She knew the medal had no magic powers—just her wishes and her imagination—but her pulse steadied a fraction.

Men shouted. Crack! A woman's wailing suddenly cut short.

A pause, followed by voices and feet scuffling on the road.

She flinched as the pounding on the gate was punctuated with tinkles from the door's chimes. The gate slammed open. Men shouted orders as they moved into the house.

No sound for several minutes.

Quiet.

Then crack! Short, sharp. Like the sound of a single firecracker. Another crack.

Something crashed.

The soldiers laughed. Fear tightened the muscles along her back. She gripped her knees, ready to rise as instinct compelled her to run back to the house. She fought it.

The door from the kitchen to the garden slammed open.

Holding the medallion and feeling the impression of the pearl and dragon's tail on her hands, she attempted to evoke magic that couldn't be there. If she were a dragon, she could make herself invisible. At least that was what her aunt's tales said.

I'm not here; please don't see me, she repeated in her mind.

The door to the shed jerked open, making the hinges cry out in distress.

One pair of boots stomped to the middle of the shed. The man shifted the boxes and crates that surrounded him.

A barrel crashed, breaking the staves. As the odor of vinegar filled the shed, she imagined the slosh of pickled cabbage sliding onto the floor.

The soldier shouted words that sounded harsh and cruel. The men standing outside the shed laughed.

Leave me alone. Please don't see me. She repeated the incantation over and over in her mind.

The soldier sloshed and slipped over to the row of boxes that hid her.

She renewed her mantra, holding onto the medallion for comfort while chiding herself—magical amulets belonged in the world of old China. When he started to lift the top box off the wall she built, fear took over.

The box he opened held nothing but excess clothing. He tossed the garments aside while Kimi held her breath. You don't see me. You don't see me. Discarded clothing rained down on her head. Didn't he realize there was an open space behind the row of boxes? That it was just an illusion?

The clothing shower ceased. The soldier tossed the box aside. Kimi shuddered at the shadow of the man's arms, seeming engorged by the light from the moon behind him. Certainly he could see her now. She didn't move.

He backed to the entrance and joined the other men. Laughter, punctuated by brief, sharp phrases, faded toward the house. Before reaching the kitchen, they stopped and shots exploded through the fragile walls of the shed.

Kimi drew her legs and arms in to form a tight ball while splinters rained down around her.

Go away. Go away.

The barrage stopped and the kitchen door slammed, dimming the noise of their bravado.

Kimi held her tense pose to a count of five hundred. No soldiers returned. She stretched her legs. Except for a dozen splinters prickling her skin, there were no more points of pain.

A few minutes later she heard rocks hammering the front of the house. A window shattered.

What had they done to Aunt Lu and Grandfather? Staying in the shed was the hardest thing she'd ever done, but running straight into the arms of the Japanese soldiers would demean Grandfather's sacrifice.

She counted again to five hundred, finally hearing the soldiers stomp back through the front gate. Sounding like a drunken party, they struck the door chimes as they passed.

Another five hundred seconds.

Standing slowly, she peered over the top of her wall of boxes. No soldiers.

The top hinge on the shed door had been pulled away so that the door lay nearly on its side. From what she could tell, no one remained in the garden.

She lifted her backpack, sliding her arms through the straps and tying the sash at her waist. Quietly she began lifting the boxes of her wall to make an exit. She stepped through, holding back a gasp as she slid on the slick vinegar and cabbage.

At the door she checked the rest of the garden, but plastered herself to the wall when she saw movement near the pond. Her heart thudded in her throat. Plaintive mewing followed the path from the pond. She took a deep breath, releasing the tension in her shoulders.

Still, no sounds came from the house.

A few steps to the kitchen—the smell of smoke. "Grandfather," she whispered. "Aunt Lu!"

Chapter Seven

Shi-lin then went to her mother and spoke of her love for Tuan.

Her mother cried. "Daughter, are there none among our kind you could love? This Tuan will break your heart. The difference in your natures will keep the innermost places in your lives apart. He will not truly know what it is to be a creature of magic, and you will never truly understand what it is to be human."

"Mother, I do not need to understand all there is to know about humans. I already know Tuan gives meaning to every day I live. When I am apart from him, my heart withers."

"What will happen to your heart when he dies, as surely he must?"

"A part of me will die with him, but I will cherish his memory, and it will fill the hole his life has left behind."

"What about Tuan's feelings, child? He will become jealous of your special powers, especially when he ages and you do not."

"When I marry him I intend to give up my dragon form and forgo use of my magic and as for aging, our love is so strong that such differences will not matter."

"Do you mean to forsake your dragon form? And how can you possibly deny your power? There are some things so fundamental to the core of existence that turning away could have unforeseen consequences. How can Tuan understand when you cannot give him a son?"

"I doubt, Mother, that the universe will collapse due to our love."

Shi-lin's mother pondered these words for a day and then called Shi-lin to her bower.

"Know, Daughter, that I love you. I would wish a different future for you. The heavens took an unusual path the day you were born, and you follow it still. May the Goddess guard your heart."

* * *

Kimi pushed through the kitchen door. She had to get Grandfather and Aunt Lu. If they were unconscious they would go to the heavens on a wisp of smoke—like barbarians.

The kitchen was a mess of broken crockery and spilled rice, scented with the spices dumped on the floor. She raced past, heading for Grandfather's room.

In a loud whisper she said, "Grandfather! Aunt Lu!"

Pale stripes of moonlight rendered a ghostly glow to the silk panels on the wall. The stalking tiger still crossed between two of the panels, its head and forepaws on one panel and its hindquarters and tail on the other. Eyes glowed fiercely in the dim light, as if ready to spring through the silk prison and sink his teeth into her.

She couldn't see flames, but the smoky odor smelled stronger.

She stepped into the dining room and froze when she saw the destruction. The table, chairs, and cushions were scattered. Shards of glass and porcelain covered the floor like broken shells on a storm-wracked beach. A smoky haze hung over the shattered remains of Aunt Lu's dishes.

A small, triangular piece of porcelain caught in her shoe. Bending to pick it up, she slid it into her jacket pocket. Adding it to the shattered pile seemed disrespectful.

She called again, "Grandfather! Aunt Lu!"

Kimi rushed through the wispy tendrils of smoke toward Grandfather's room. Her eyes stung and her throat filled with smoke as she bent low and plunged inside. She gagged on the putrid blend of feces, urine, and blood overpowering the smell of burning paper.

Oh, no! "Grandfather, where are you?"

Covering her nose, she stepped farther into the room and saw the small fire in the corner where books had been tossed. Her whole body screamed with the need to flee the smoky room.

But she had to find Grandfather.

She checked both sides of his bed, lifting the broken remainder of the carved screen with its delicate crane. She found him sprawled on the floor behind his desk, only a few feet away from the fire that now climbed the wall.

No! It cannot be! She dropped to one knee.

Grandfather lay on his back. A single stripe of moonlight crossed his face. One arm stretched out to the side, his fingers curving gently toward the ceiling. She willed him to blink, to turn to her and chide her for not following his orders.

She touched his shoulder. "Grandfather?"

He didn't move.

Charcoal-colored dust radiated from the center of a small circle in the middle of his forehead. A single trail of red, so dark it was almost black, flowed down his temple. It disappeared behind his ear to join a thick puddle surrounding his head.

Kimi touched his cold cheek—so cold it should have been hard like stone, but it felt soft and papery. She flinched, snatching her hand back.

A hole opened in her heart, and all her feelings fell through.

Coughing, she hugged her knees and swayed. Anguish rose within her, spilling through her eyes. Sobs wracked her so hard she struggled to catch her breath.

She couldn't let Grandfather burn.

Kneeling behind him, she slid her arms under his shoulders and pulled him partway off the ground. His head lolled back so that blood slid down her arms. She tightened her grip and dragged him into the hall. The light from the fire cast her shadow against the far wall of the hallway. Already she could feel the temper of the heat, rising to steal everything that mattered.

She continued pulling him toward the back door, checking over her shoulder every few steps, navigating a path through the destruction.

As she passed her bedroom, she could see none of her things among the litter scattered on the floor, only linens and fabrics and other items one might store in an empty room. Aunt Lu and Grandfather had carefully removed all traces of her. It was as though Kimi had never been—she was a ghost, a shadow, a nothing.

Pulling Grandfather through the main hallway she passed the ancestor shrine. It was in pieces, the ribbons and papers burnt, the plaques broken. Fists clenching and pressure building behind her eyes, she wished the ancestors could take up arms and defend their honor.

She grunted, sliding Grandfather's body through the debris, stopping every few feet to cough and adjust her grip.

Her sense of outrage blossomed as she dragged Grandfather. These cruel men touched the little things that were part of her life. Even if she had never cared for the ivory elephant lying broken on the floor, it seemed precious now. The soldiers had destroyed more than dishes and vases. They had soiled her soul with their disgusting hands.

She looked down on her grandfather's face at the soft lines she knew so well, tears dropping from her cheeks. She brushed her sweaty and tear-stained face, adjusted her grip under his arms and continued through the family room, followed by billows of smoke.

Her breath caught in a gasp. Stunned by the destruction in the kitchen when she'd entered the house, she hadn't noticed Aunt Lu's foot protruding beneath the curtain covering the pantry alcove. Dizziness robbed her of all strength. She let go of Grandfather's shoulders and leaned against the frame of the door to let the weakness pass.

"Aunt Lu..." Kimi's voice fell as her last fragile thread of hope died.

No movement, not even a flinch.

Kimi hurried to the pantry and pulled the curtain aside. Aunt Lu's head and shoulders were bent over her lap. Splatters of blood and brain matter dotted the pantry wall. Chunks of shattered glass and peach fragments completed the gruesome mix. The odors of peach juice, gunpowder, and feces made Kimi retch.

Aunt Lu's hair didn't quite hide the gaping wound in the back of her head. A ribbon of blood had flowed down the side of her aunt's neck and jaw and across the front of her light blue blouse, filling her lap with a gelid pool of dark blood.

Oh, Aunt Lu!

Kimi brushed her fingers along Aunt Lu's cheek. It was as cold as Grandfather's. Like her grandfather, a single shot marred her forehead. Aunt Lu looked older in death. Her cheeks and mouth sagged, and lines around her mouth and eyes showed deeply in the shadows. It seemed as though she had kept her skin firm by sheer force of will.

Grief fell over Kimi like a shroud. Anger followed. If only Xiao had been here. He could have carried them to safety. Was this her special destiny? To see her family killed? To be an orphan again? Pressure filled Kimi's head. Her hands tingled.

She went back to where she'd left Grandfather at the entry to the kitchen and slid her arms under his shoulders with newfound strength. Clearing a path through the debris as best she could, Kimi pulled Grandfather out the back door and into the garden, all the way to the pool where she hoped he would be safe from the fire.

Kimi returned to the house and dragged Aunt Lu from the kitchen to rest beside her brother.

The smell of the fire got stronger; she could see flames rising above the roof over the bedrooms. She looked at the pond and thought about the bucket in the shed and realized the futility of trying to put the fire out.

By the light of the burning house, she looked around the garden and spotted a flat area between the pond and an oak tree. She retrieved the garden spade from where she had left it when cleaning out the storage shed.

If someone were watching, she would look like a demon digging through the fires of hell, working through the packed soil in the light of the blazing inferno.

After two hours, the holes were barely deep enough, but her arms could not lift another scoop of soil or cut away the tendril of another root. In the meantime, the fire had swallowed the house, leaving little more than a glowing skeleton.

She dragged Aunt Lu's and Grandfather's bodies into the common grave, shame making her motions clumsy. She gently closed her grandfather's dead eyes, straightened his robe, and moved his arms so they rested naturally at his side. With gentle strokes she removed the blood staining her aunt's cheeks and smoothed back her hair. These were the only funeral preparations she could make. She hoped Grandfather's ancestors would not reject him because he was not buried in a coffin with a yellow cloth covering his face.

Begging Aunt Lu's gods for mercy, she sprinkled the first handfuls of dirt onto their bodies. When she finished scooping the soil and packing the grave, she covered it with leaves. Hopefully the Japanese wouldn't notice.

Then Kimi lowered herself to the base of the oak tree and watched as the moon disappeared behind the mountains, taking away its pure light. She could not rant and wail as the women normally did, fearing the Japanese would hear her. Her heart felt crushed from the pressure of so much grief locked inside her.

What good was destiny if she could not protect the people who matter? She should never have listened to them. Despite what Aunt Lu said, they weren't done living. Kimi had been a foundling, yet they had loved her as a daughter and given up their lives for her. She had to make herself worthy of their sacrifice.

Her exhaustion worked like Grandfather's pills. She didn't notice when she fell asleep.

She awoke from a nightmare with a panic-driven start. What if the Japanese return? Her hands clenched the medallion, but this time it didn't comfort her. Cold sweat dotted her forehead. The sky was still coal black; the only light came from the glowing embers of her house. She didn't hear any Japanese soldiers, but that didn't mean they weren't there.

The dream had been so vivid. Its horror clung tightly as though she were still standing in front of the soldier. She had stood in the garden beside the carp pond. She wore the pack and had been ready to leave. The soldier came from the kitchen door, calling to her with foreign words.

She had frozen. Her legs felt like sticks. Her mouth was so dry she couldn't scream or cry for help. It didn't matter. There was no one who could help her. They were all dead.

The soldier raised his gun, pointing it straight at her.

He took one slow step, then another, looking neither right nor left.

Step. Step. Until he was right before her.

The gun pointed inches from her head.

Panic pushed at her limbs, trying to make them run, but she couldn't move. Pressure built behind her eyes and her hands tingled.

Fear confined her, controlled her. A small place at the back of her mind got angry at her helplessness. The anger grew until her arms and legs felt strong.

She wouldn't let him kill her. She had to make him stop.

With a surge of will, her arms moved.

She reached out, but it wasn't her hand that pushed the gun away. It was a beast's claw—five long, black talons curved like scimitars from a knob-like hand and thickly-scaled arm.

It struck the soldier in the chest, knocking him to the ground. The soldier's eyes bulged, and his mouth opened wide as he let out a terrified scream.

In her dream, Kimi turned and fled.

The nightmare resonated in her waking mind even as she looked around the garden and saw the black night beginning to yield to the faint grey of morning. Soft light crept into the crevices of the rocks and branches of the trees.

She listened carefully for sounds of soldiers and heard only silence. The dream had seemed so real. Her mind was playing tricks on her.

When she pulled Grandfather's garden jacket around her thin chest, a sharp jab scraped her side. She found a palm-sized spike of blue and white willow porcelain in the bottom of the pocket. The wedge from the center of a plate showed the severed head of the Goddess Kuan Yin and a sliver of the pavilion that sheltered her. Kimi put the shard back in her pocket. It might be a silly talisman, but it was all she had left of her home.

For a moment a flood of thanksgiving filled her. She was alive. Guilt cut off the thought like a cleaver. Grandfather and Aunt Lu had paid for her life with their own.

Crack!

Kimi jumped. She turned toward the sound just in time to see a cloud of smoke and ash billow up from the ruins of the house. Charred wooden beams now leaned into its center where the courtyard had been. Smoke and ash covered the timbers until a flaky bit peeled away, revealing the coals the fire had left when it ravaged the house.

No soldiers in sight, but she needed to leave in a hurry. She had promised Grandfather she would go to Xiao. Even though she felt abandoned by him, she had to keep her promise. And someday, somehow, she would strike back at the Japanese who murdered her family. She might not be able to kill them all, but despite Aunt Lu's warnings about going to the Ten Hells of Anger, she would take at least two Japanese soldiers with her. One for Aunt Lu and one for Grandfather.

It seemed a lifetime since her midnight waking. She watched the swelling yellow sky where the sun would soon rise. If all went well, there would be five more sunrises before she reached Xiao's home, but she couldn't let the Japanese get ahead of her. Most likely they'd made camp in the fields outside Kaisun. They'd wake soon. She needed to be far away before they began to march.

Adjusting the backpack, she crept away from the ruins of what used to be her house.

Chapter Eight

Before the month was over, Shi-lin appeared to Tuan in
dragon form, her azure scales shining in the sunlight. She stood tall
and proud, her arching neck covered in glistening armament tipped
with the faintest hyacinth and gold that filled the sky just before dawn.
Each scale deepened to the darkest sapphire of a moonlit night where it
touched her body.

On her head a crown of horns arched gracefully from her
brows. A soft blue pearl rested between gold-flecked eyes. As she
reached out to him with five obsidian claws closed to a point, his hand
touched hers.

He was not afraid but watched her with wonder. Then she
transformed to the woman's shape he knew so there would be no
secrets between them.

He neither bowed nor wept. Rather, his whole being shone
with the light of his loving.

She could see the question in his eyes. Had she come to explain
why she could not marry him?

"Shi-lin, you have returned to me."

She stepped close and took his hand, doubt heavy in her own mind. "I have come, but knowing what I am, do you still wish for me to be your wife?"

He took her into his arms and held her close. "Were you a demon and my soul in peril, still I would want you to share my life." Even so, a worry creased his brow. "Will you not tire of an insignificant human? I cannot shower you with riches or give you a life of ease."

"Tuan, I do not require jewels or comforts. I have been beside you even when you could not see me. Your life is beautiful in its simplicity. With you, I am the wealthiest woman in heaven or on earth."

He stepped back taking both her hands. "Shi-lin, I pledge to you my spirit and my soul, not only for this life but for all of time. Not even death will keep me from loving you."

"Dearest Tuan, my soul rests in your palms, now and always."

She committed his words to memory together with the depth of their meaning, hearing the echo of her own feelings. She called the deep magic to make her more than a semblance of a woman, so she could share joy and pain in the ways that only those of flesh can feel.

* * *

Being a wife was hard for Shi-lin at first. Though for years she had watched people as they went about their daily tasks, she learned that making jam was much more involved than cooking berries with sugar. Tuan patiently taught her how to wash clothes, mend shoes, and how to harvest roots from the forest.

Once she became proficient in household duties, she rushed through her days so that she had time to herself. She built a small garden on the side of the hill just beyond their house while Tuan tended their fields in the afternoons. She tamed a brook so that it ran down the stony course she laid for it. She took small trees and flowering plants from the forest and placed them to overlook the clearing that led from their home in a broad sweep down to the lake.

* * *

Kimi approached the road, crouching down beside the skeletal ruins of the gate. She peered into the smoky dregs of a waning night, looking right to the road north and left toward Kaisun, straining all her senses.

A faint thu-thunk… thu-thunk… came from the direction of the town. Her thoughts scattered as the sound moved steadily closer. Between the beats of the muffled clanking, she heard a child wailing.

"Hush," a man's voice said. "Don't make so much noise."

The wails grew louder.

"You'll wake the soldiers. Hurry, boy. Keep up."

She recognized the baker's stern voice and released her pent-up breath.

Kimi stepped from behind the smoldering gatepost, picking her way carefully through the ash-covered timbers.

Peering around the corner, she saw Mister Cho and his nephew, Hachi, walking down the center of the road. With one hand the baker braced a large flour sack flung over his shoulder.

With his other hand, Cho gripped Hachi, who was also burdened with a small sack. Cho half-dragged the boy in his wake.

Flour smudged Cho's beard and dusted the front of his jacket. In his haste, he had pulled his jacket on over his apron, not even taking the time to button it. The baker's potbelly pushed through the opening of the jacket; the apron hung nearly to his knees. His queue had loosened, and his pillbox hat sat askew. Hachi dressed no better, wore a jacket sized for a boy twice as old.

Mister Cho stopped in the road when he saw her. The flour sack gave a clank as it settled. He was fleeing with his pots.

Hachi continued blindly forward until Cho yanked his arm. The boy whimpered.

Kimi didn't blame him. What heavenly injustice placed the poor child's fate into this cruel man's hands?

Why would Cho be taking Hachi? Cho hated children. Hachi's parents must be dead. Poor child. And he was only six. Kimi knew all too well what it was like to grow up as an orphan, even in a home where people loved you. The child's longing to have his mother hold him would never go away.

The baker scowled. "Why are you still here? Don't you know the soldiers are taking the young women?" For a moment the scowl melted. His face blanched as white as the flour on his apron.

"I saw them take your friend, Mei. They weren't kind to her, nor to her dead baby when they cut it out."

Not Mei! Her baby! What else had Cho seen? Kimi's imagination sent a rapid flicker of images, each worse than the previous. Grandfather had been right to worry about her safety. Having heard the soldier's malicious laughter in the night, she cringed at the thought of being caught by them. More than once she'd wished Mei bad luck. But not this. Never this. She touched the medallion, trying to ease the pain.

Kimi looked back toward the town, squinting, hoping for others—maybe a young mother to take charge of Hachi.

"Don't bother looking. We're all that's left. Never imagined there could be so much blood." He raised a shoe. "No amount of soap will get these clean."

Kimi leaned forward until her face was inches from Cho's. "That's all you can think about? Your shoes?"

"You would too if yours were soaked in blood. They will dry hard and crack, rubbing my feet at the creases."

Kimi fumed. Her hands tingled, but she took a deep breath and let the anger float away at the sight of Hachi crouched in the road covering his ears with his hands. Cho had a firm grasp of one hand. Hachi lowered the sack to the ground with his other.

"No you don't, boy," Cho said, jerking the boy up by the arm. "Don't even think of putting the bag down. We're leaving. This is as much rest as you'll get until the sun sets."

"No! This isn't right." Kimi marched up to Hachi, took the bag from him, and dropped it on the ground three feet away. "Let's go, Hachi."

She took his little hand, but Cho tugged on the other one, stretching Hachi like the wishbone of a duck.

Kimi let go. "You don't want this boy! Why put him through this misery?"

"I need an apprentice; this boy will do. I am his only living relative."

The fire in Kimi's chest burned to be let out. Again, she held it back. Aunt Lu's gods must be laughing at her foolishness. She would go with Cho to protect Hachi, but once in Pianshan, she would find a way to escape from Cho and take Hachi with her. Only a crazy person would go into the mountains with a small boy this time of year, but she couldn't bear to think of him living under Cho's rule.

"All right, you win." She picked up the bag Hachi had been carrying and tied it to the strap of her pack. It was heavier than it seemed.

"Careful, girl. Those are my knives and rolling pins."

Kimi ticked off her demands. "I will also carry your bag if Hachi needs to be carried. We will stop when he needs to rest. Someone will have water to sell; you will buy it."

With his mouth hanging open, Cho said, "Who put you in charge? You will steal my pots and start your own bakery. That's your real purpose."

Kimi spat in the dust. "And outrun you to Pianshan carrying both bags and Hachi? If you are in such a hurry, let's go."

Cho had to get in the last word. "It's good we are getting away before the sun's fully up, but you must keep up. I assume you have food and money in that pack of yours?"

"I have a little money, not much. I don't know how much food Aunt Lu packed."

"Well, at least you have your own blanket." Snatching Hachi's hand, Cho stood straight like a great general. "Come, boy, we need to keep moving."

Hachi looked back over his sagging shoulder. Kimi shivered at the sight of the haunted emptiness on the boy's tear-streaked, dusty face. His attempt to use a sleeve to wipe his nose had left a shiny smear on one chubby cheek. Kimi quickly caught up and gave his hand a gentle squeeze.

"My name is Kimi. I am sure your mā would want you to have a friend."

Hachi's chin quivered, but he straightened his back and stuck his chest out. Kimi admired the little boy's iron will.

"Kaisun… What happened?" she asked Cho, quickening her steps to keep pace with the baker.

An early morning breeze laden with chill, damp moisture blew across the lake. Cho shivered. "You don't want to know. Trust me. You don't want to know."

But she needed to know. She looked back in the direction they had come, searching for signs of the Japanese soldiers who must be on the move by now. All she saw were shadows from low clouds blown by the wind. Perhaps the soldiers had headed in a different direction. She could hope, but that wasn't likely. She struggled to walk faster, but her feet felt as if they were mired in clay. "Are you sure no one else is coming? Surely others managed to survive."

"None that I saw. I found the boy hiding in the butcher's storehouse, wedged between two sides of pork. It's a miracle he lived. The lucky few who left yesterday morning are all that's left of Kaisun."

Hachi's thin voice pierced the air. "Is my mā dead? Where is she? Will I see her soon?"

"You'll see her all too soon if we don't hurry," Mister Cho muttered.

Kimi bit her lip at Mister Cho's cruelty, but it wasn't the time to tell Hachi his parents were dead. The child would figure it out soon enough.

"Didn't anyone try to stop the soldiers?" Kimi asked, hoping to divert Hachi's attention away from his question.

For a moment Cho looked fierce. "One hundred tradesmen against a full phalanx of Japanese soldiers? A few tried to fight, but..." he looked at Hachi. "It didn't go well."

Kimi clutched the medallion and wished somehow that Cho's words could be unsaid. She hurried to keep pace while Hachi shuffled to keep up.

"It was a terrible sight." Cho said.

Jerking his hand away from Cho, Hachi turned to Kimi, his cheeks flushed with emotion. "I saw it. The butcher was brave. The soldiers shot him when he ran into the street with his sword. He killed a soldier before he fell down dead. I want to kill a soldier just like he did."

The butcher dead? The kind man who gave Kimi the best cuts of meat? Perhaps his valiant act would earn him the chance of another life—if there were gods. She wanted to shout to all of Kaisun—see what your gods let happen?

Kimi grew nauseated as the scene repeated itself in her mind. Hachi might be excited now, but it would haunt him later in his sleep. She wanted to kill the Japanese, too. Another stiff breeze lifted off the lake, pushing smoky tendrils of hair across her face. Oh, Grandfather! Aunt Lu!

Cho's voice held a note of derision. "The butcher had no sense. He should have found a way to hide his father, but the gods will probably reward him for bravery."

At least the butcher had done something. Where had she been? Hiding in the shed.

She would never forgive the Japanese. Not for the deaths of Grandfather and Aunt Lu. Not for what they had done to Mei and her unborn baby. Not for robbing the kind butcher of his future. What good was she to anyone if she couldn't protect the people she loved? She tried to force those thoughts from her mind and put all her strength into getting away. Hachi would slow her down, but she couldn't leave the boy in Cho's unkind hands.

The trio marched forward while the sun rose to full morning. Through the sound of her rushing heart, she listened for the beat of feet on the road. Refugees from other towns joined them, coming from the narrow paths leading to their farms. The road became choked with carts, oxen, and straggling families. Discarded items lined the road, refugees lightening their load so they could outpace the Japanese. So far, they had met only one farmer heading to Kaisun. Kimi told the farmer to turn back, but he stubbornly continued on, muttering that she was being hysterical.

Hachi interrupted her thoughts. "How much longer until we see my mā?"

Cho spit into the dusty road. "Hush boy. Your mother is waiting for us. We'll see her soon."

Doubt shadowed Hachi's face. To distract him, Kimi said, "Did you know that a man named Hachi was a great general? Are you going to be brave and strong when you grow up?"

His head bobbed up and down.

Good. He would need that determination.

"I bet you will be." As soon as they got clear of the Japanese, Kimi would take him into her lap and tell him the truth about his parents.

Around noon, they stopped for a moment to rest, drink water, and eat the apples Aunt Lu had packed for Kimi. Not much time to linger. They would have to walk quite a few hours until they could rest again.

Walking along the rocky verge of the road, they bypassed the clot of refugees. Ahead of them was a nearly empty stretch of roadway. When they reached high spots, a large group of refugees came into view several miles ahead. The thin line of stragglers behind them looked like a dragon's tail curving around a bend in the road. Kimi shuddered, thinking of the people who hadn't made it out of Kaisun at all. She longed for the strength to sweep Hachi into her arms and run all the way to Pianshan where there would be Chinese soldiers to protect them.

Kimi plodded forward, listening to the other refugees asking about loved ones left behind. Every time Hachi slowed down, Cho shouted at him.

When Kimi looked over her shoulder again, a cloud of dust on the horizon made her gasp. Could it be the Japanese soldiers? Cho saw it too, his face expression growing hard. He jerked Hachi's arm. "We must go faster. Do you want the Japanese soldiers to catch you?"

Why did the fates allow the disagreeable Mister Cho to live while Grandfather and Aunt Lu died? The thought made her too angry to cry.

Mister Cho finally stopped when Hachi stumbled. The stream of refugees continued around them.

"You can carry my bag. I'll carry the boy." Without a moment's hesitation, he slung the flour sack off his shoulder and with a clanking and banging of pots, dumped it on the ground at her feet. Bending, he told the boy to climb on his back.

"I don't have to walk anymore?" Hachi's face lit up. With eyes full of hope he looked at Kimi. "Can I have some water, too?"

Cho grabbed the boy's shoulder and turned him to face the road behind. He pointed to the cloud of dust. "We don't have time for water now. Those are the Japanese. Get on my back." He spun the boy to face the road ahead and bent low.

Fàng pì! Kimi longed to tell Cho what she thought of him. Instead she helped Hachi climb onto the grumbling baker's back.

Hachi looked at her with relief on his face.

Lifting Cho's makeshift bag, she slipped her head under the knot. The pots bumped noisily against her pack. His bag was heavier than hers, especially with the second bag of knives and rolling pins. The knot dug cruelly into the soft flesh between her neck and shoulder. She lifted the knot and raised the collar of her jacket, freeing the medallion so it didn't bite into her. Maybe she could make it as far as the bend in the road far ahead.

With the added strain on her shoulders and back, she fell behind. "Mister Cho," she called when the distance between them had grown.

He turned and glared at her, his nostrils flaring. "Keep up, girl. You're no better than the boy," his voice growled

Kimi ground her teeth and reminded herself that she was staying with him for Hachi's sake.

Cho stared at her for a moment. When he resumed his walk, his pace slowed enough for Kimi to keep up.

Chapter Nine

When all was done to her satisfaction, she took Tuan to see what she had wrought. "I have made this place of beauty for us to share, but it is incomplete. I do not know how to fashion a bench."

"I will show you." He taught her the working of wood. Together they made a bench as beautiful as her garden. In the early mornings, they watched the birds take flight. In the evenings, they watched the deer come to the lake.

* * *

It was getting dark when they encountered a slow-moving group of refugees. A young couple with two small children pushed a wheelbarrow packed so full that the load threatened to topple any second. An ox plodded ahead, pulling a larger cart packed more sensibly and allowing space for the old grandmother to ride. Kimi didn't recognize the travelers.

The people looked at Kimi with tired eyes as she slipped past, but other than a nod, they said nothing. They shared her sorrows; they could do nothing about them. She could see it in the troubled faces of the elders and the wide, staring eyes of the children. She wondered if she looked as shattered.

The next time Kimi fell behind, Cho stopped.

He set the boy down and scanned the road behind them. Kimi followed his gaze. The dust cloud had disappeared. The Japanese must have stopped for the night. She felt little relief.

Hachi collapsed in the road and pulled off his shoes. Both heels oozed blood from broken blisters. "It hurts," he said in a voice so soft Kimi had to strain to hear it.

Kimi sighed. "Mr. Cho, we need to find a cart for Hachi and your bag."

Cho spat on the ground. The disgust in his voice could fill a bucket. "Even if someone would let us ride with them, a cart is even slower than you."

She could hear Aunt Lu's voice in her head saying "Respect, Kimi, respect, even if he doesn't deserve it." Kimi reached up and touched her medallion, her patience wearing thin.

"Besides, they would expect me to pay them," Cho said. "I have no money for such things."

Fàng pì! She didn't think the small coins in her pocket would pay for a ride, but she thought of the silver pieces Grandfather had wrapped so carefully. When the break was over, she slung his bag onto her back again, reversed directions, and approached the cart with the old grandmother riding atop.

She heard the end of one of the monkey stories as she approached the father. The children's haggard looks brightened as they listened to the impossible tales of the magical and powerful Monkey King. They might be made-up stories, but

Monkey could defeat large forces with his simple cudgel and magical tricks—even defeat the gods. He gave courage and hope where there was little to be found.

"May I help you?" the father asked, setting the wheelbarrow down.

Kimi pointed to Hachi. "Is it possible that our little boy could ride on your cart, even for a little while?"

"He seems light enough, but I have the ox carrying as much as he can."

The man didn't seem to be soliciting a bribe, but money might still make a difference.

"I have some money. I can pay you to take Hachi and also for anything left behind to make room for him."

Tapping his finger on his cheek, the man looked toward his wife who nodded a fraction.

Kimi set Cho's bag down. Cho had disappeared, possibly to relieve himself, so Kimi turned her back and walked a few paces away from the man. She retrieved the rolled-up scroll of money from the bottom of her pack, freed two silver pieces, and then pushed the roll of money back to the bottom.

The man took the two silver bars, eyes peering up between furrowed brows. "This is too much. I'm only taking the boy as far as Pianshan, yes?"

"Only as far as Pianshan. You'll need the money to start over."

Kimi watched as tension slid from the wife's face. She bowed from the waist with her hands clasped in front. "Thank you."

After removing a small chest, the man helped a grinning Hachi take a seat beside the grandmother.

Cho had returned on silent feet making Kimi wonder if he'd seen the silver. He didn't act like it, but she wished she could be sure. Impatient as usual, he pointed to his bag on the ground and motioned for Kimi to pick it up. He fetched the bag of knives. It was just like Cho to take the lighter load. He reached over the side of the cart and dumped the bag of knives and rolling pins on Hachi's lap.

Hadn't Cho heard the father saying that the load was too heavy for the ox? Hadn't he seen this family discarding their chest to accommodate Hachi? The father said nothing to Cho. Maybe the bag of knives didn't weight much. Still, Cho's behavior angered her.

She dropped the bag of pots in the road and took a few steps. Cho cleared his throat and pointed. She thought about leaving the bag of pots and running ahead on her own. Maybe the man and woman would take care of Hachi with the money she'd given them. But no. She gave Hachi one look and knew she couldn't do that. Disgusted with Cho and disgusted with herself for giving in, she picked up the bag and strained forward.

The ox leaned in to his traces and the cart lurched forward. The family followed behind—passing the discarded set of drawers. With the bag of pots in hand, Kimi followed the cart while Cho walked alongside.

Hachi seemed captivated by the monkey stories the man told. He described Monkey's magical cudgel. It shrank to the size of a sewing needle that Monkey tucked behind his ear until he needed it.

"Monkey loved playing jokes on the gods. One day he stole some of Lao Tsu's golden elixir of life. The Jade God got so angry he sent an army to bring Monkey back to stand trial."

"What happened?" Hachi asked. "Did they catch him?"

"No, they didn't catch him, but it was close. Monkey was trapped at the base of a mountain. He reached behind his ear, changing the pin into a cudgel. Using his cudgel to perform tricks that let him disappear and reappear—magic he'd stolen from the gods—he utterly defeated the large army against him."

Hachi waved his arms about with his own imaginary cudgel in imitation of Monkey's antics.

Perhaps these tales would give Hachi courage. Too bad they were only stories. Kimi wished she could disappear and reappear, and defeat the Japanese in a single blow.

Hachi sneezed. His nose had been running since they left Kaisun. Now his cheeks looked like little red apples. If he got sick, she could do nothing for him.

The pace was slow, but without carrying a double load or stopping frequently to allow Hachi to catch up, they made good time.

At one point Kimi fell in step with an old woman. The woman smiled, face ancient, wrinkled like a withered apple and just as brown. Her blue jacket with embroidered cranes had once been beautiful but now was patched and faded with age. Yet the graceful way she walked didn't fit Kimi's idea of an old peasant woman. She looked like the same old woman Kimi had seen in the Kaisun market the morning before the Japanese attack. How could she have walked such a long way?

"Where are you going, child?" the woman asked. "Do you have family in Pianshan?"

"No, I'm just going through Pianshan. I want to get away from the Japanese. They killed my family."

"Do not concern yourself about the Japanese this evening. They have stopped for the night."

How could the woman know that? But then Kimi recalled thinking the same thing. The thought gave her a small amount of comfort.

"Once you escape the Japanese where will you go?"

"Into the mountains." Kimi answered. "I intend to take the boy with me,"

"Oh?"

"Hachi may be Mister Cho's nephew, but he treats the boy like a dog. I can't watch Cho strike Hachi anymore. The child needs tenderness. I know. I'm an orphan, too. Besides, the Japanese won't go into the mountains. We should be safe."

The old woman nodded. "The boy will need you. Retribution is strong in both of you. You can't kill them all, you know. The soldiers may become tired of killing by the time they arrive in Pianshan."

Kimi remembered the soldiers' crude laughter outside her home. These men wouldn't tire of their cruelty. She thought of how things might have been different if Xiao had stayed to help get Grandfather and Aunt Lu to safety.

As though she'd heard Kimi's thoughts, the woman said, "No. If they are to keep what they have won, they will remember that farmers, bakers, apothecaries, and the rest keep them fed and comfortable. Some will remember their own grandfathers when they see the faces of the dead men."

Kimi felt strange comfort from the woman's words, even if she didn't believe them. She longed with all her heart to turn back to Kaisun and find everything the way it had always been—Mei's harsh comments, the gossiping in front of the laundry, readying the garden for winter, doing errands for Aunt Lu.

"Do you have family in the mountains?" the woman asked.

"No. Not really. Grandfather told me I should go to the home of a friend—a former student of his." The thought of Grandfather made her blink away tears.

"I made a hiding place, but they wouldn't go. Instead of hiding out myself, I should have carried Grandfather with me. Aunt Lu would have come then. They are dead because of me."

The old woman placed her withered hand on Kimi's shoulder. "Do not blame yourself. It was their time to die." The woman's hand, light as a beetle, soothed Kimi.

"What is your name, child?"

"Tengshe." Why did she say that name?

"What a lovely name. Your grandfather's student, do you know him?"

Moved by the woman's tenderness, Kimi answered. "I thought I knew him, but perhaps not. Xiao is a scholar. Now all he wants to be is a farmer."

"Ah." The woman nodded and turned her face toward Kimi. "So, you do not wish to live with a farmer. That must be difficult."

Kimi's mind hurt. She wanted to honor Grandfather's instructions, but she wanted to do more with her life than work on a farm. Once the Japanese left she would convince Xiao to go back to the city—any city—even if all he did was teach.

The woman chuckled. "You have spirit, girl. I think you will need it. But do not be so sure of your friend's intentions. Perhaps there is more to him than you know."

"Perhaps," Kimi replied, doubting it.

The woman smiled, causing her wrinkles to deepen. "You will have an interesting life, child. Just wait and see. In time you will believe passionately in what you now so vehemently deny."

Kimi opened her mouth to ask the woman to explain what she meant. How could she possibly know?

Cho yelled at her to catch up. Kimi nodded to the woman and moved ahead on sore feet.

When Kimi looked back, the woman had disappeared. Odd. She had disappeared in Kaisun's market, too. Who was she?

Perplexed, Kimi looked at the cart to check on Hachi. He wasn't there.

"Where's Hachi?" Kimi shouted as she rushed to the back of the cart.

"I thought he was with you," the man said.

"Did you see where he went?"

"Skipping back to see you, brandishing an imaginary cudgel."

No sign of a small boy in the crowd of people now on the road. Kimi moved into the throng, Cho shouting furiously after her.

"Hachi's missing," she shouted over her shoulder.

What had the old woman said? Retribution was strong in him. Would he have gone back to fight the Japanese with his imaginary sword? She headed straight through the cluster of refugees, seeking a high spot where one small person could be seen walking south, opposite the flow of traffic.

He had not made it far. Not even to the edge of the crowd of refugees. And the old woman was right. There was no sign of the Japanese troops. They must have made camp for the night. That is unless they had left the road and were planning to attack them by surprise.

With that thought in mind, Kimi raced after Hachi, catching him up in her arms. Not wanting to scold, she tried to sound calm. "Hachi, where are you going? You frightened me."

"I am going to get my honor back. The Monkey King fought the Imperial Jade's army all by himself! I am just as brave." He waved his imaginary sword in the air.

"Now is not the time." She tugged on his arm.

Hachi anchored his feet to the road, jerking away from her grasp. "I won't go with you."

"I know you're brave, but it takes more than one boy to defeat an army. How many people do you think the Japanese killed in Kaisun? Thousands, probably. We need to think of a better way."

"I thought you were my friend."

"I am your friend. I want you to kill dozens of Japanese and still live to kill more, but I don't want you to get hurt."

Hachi stomped his foot. "I want the Japanese gone now!"

She smoothed back the loose hairs blowing into his tear-filled eyes. "So do I, Hachi. So do I."

The cart was still where she'd left it. A fuming Cho berated the man and anyone else nearby for letting Kimi steal his apprentice. When Kimi and Hachi approached, he turned his wrath on them, cuffing Hachi on the ears. Skewering them with his pointed finger, spittle flew as he shouted at Kimi. "Thief! How dare you take my apprentice and run."

"How could I have run away from you? We're all on the same road going the same direction. I was looking for Hachi, your precious apprentice. You could at least thank me for bringing him back."

Hachi climbed back up onto the cart with promises to stay put. The man picked up the wheelbarrow, the ox moved forward and they rejoined the stream of refugees.

Cho wasn't willing to stop for the night when the cart pulled over to the side of the road. He made Hachi climb down and ordered Kimi to keep going.

Kimi, Cho, and Hachi walked until the sun fell below the line of the mountains and an hour past that. When they finally stopped, Kimi was beyond pain. Thirst and hunger beat at the edges of her consciousness. She had nearly forgotten why she was fleeing or where she was going. Her destination had become the next curve in the road, the next farm, the next tree. She had quit looking up at the mountains; it disheartened her to see they seemed no closer.

They stopped at the edge of a farm, just where the rutted farm track broke away from the road. She crumpled to the hard ground beside her pack. A cricket chirped in the grass behind her. Just moving to the softer grass would take more energy than she had left. Her blisters were shooting points of pain.

Hachi's hands were in tight fists, his lips pressed tight. Deep lines appeared to be permanently imprinted on his forehead. He huddled at her side, a finger stuck into his mouth for comfort. He patted Kimi's hand. "It will be better soon."

His words pierced Kimi's heart. How could she tell him it would never be better? She stroked Hachi's hair as he curled up beside her pack. Kimi unfastened her blanket and put it over him when he fell asleep.

Mister Cho settled in the grass with his bag open beside him. Drawing two buns out of his bag, he handed one to Kimi. "Don't get too comfortable. We'll be up well before dawn."

She ate the bun slowly, saving half for Hachi.

Before she finished her half of the bun, she fell into exhausted sleep, telling herself it would just be for an hour or two.

Kimi woke in a panic, her eyes opening to early morning light. Rustling sounds had intruded on her dream. Had the Japanese caught up with them? She listened. No guttural mutterings of the Japanese soldiers or the clanking of their guns. Only silence.

Still, something was terribly wrong.

Chapter Ten

*Each month Tuan would go, and each month she feared for his
safe return, regretting her vow to remain as a human.*

*In the month of the Orchid, Tuan returned from the city with
his cart laden with a large, stone lantern. They placed it beside the
bench so they could sit in the evenings, warmed by the fire at its center
and watch the stars come out.*

*Then he taught her how to craft a flute to match his own. In
the evenings, they discovered ways to blend the voices of their music as
they learned to blend the rhythm of their days.*

* * *

Kimi sprang to her feet. "Mister Cho. What are you
doing?"

He sneered but didn't say anything.

He was taking her money! She lunged for the pack.
Catching hold of one of the straps, she gave it a hard tug. Cho
tugged even harder, stepping back and dragging her with it like
a helpless child.

He slammed the pack into her chest, causing her to land hard on her back. The air whooshed out of her lungs, and she lay stunned.

Hachi stirred, mumbling in a sweet groggy voice. Kimi struggled to get up, taking deep breaths.

Mister Cho turned the pack upside down, spilling the contents. Tossing the bag aside, he stooped to paw through her things. In seconds, he stood and crowed. "Aha, this is what I was looking for." He held up the folded panel that held her grandfather's money, all but the few coins she'd put in her pockets. She heard the chink of silver.

"That's mine!" Both her temper and her voice rose. "You have no right to take it."

She launched herself toward the baker. He shoved the cloth containing the silver into the large pocket of his apron. She tried to grab the money, but he pushed her into the dirt again.

Hachi whimpered. He moved away as Mister Cho loomed over Kimi and jabbed his finger in her face.

"No, you are wrong, girl," Cho yelled. "I have every right to it. For years my taxes have been given to the magistrates, including your grandfather. Money paid to protect me. Where was the protection when the soldiers came? Where were the Empress's toy soldiers?"

"Grandfather did protect you. Kaisun had rice during the famine, didn't it?"

She stood and leaped toward him, but he stepped aside, causing her to stumble.

"Thief!" she screamed. The early morning travelers turned their heads briefly before continuing their journey. Of course no one would help, not when it looked like she was having a fight with her grandfather. Besides, Cho would accuse her of trying to steal from him.

Anger made her palms tingle and itch. Her eyesight narrowed until she could see the smallest details sharply, such as the crumbs from the bun he'd eaten the night before. When she reached out, she saw the shadow of a clawed, scaled hand outlining her arm.

Hachi's squeal barely penetrated. Cho scrambled back on his hands and feet.

Fàng pì! She had scared Hachi. The scales faded.

"Corruption. Deceit. That's what my taxes bought." Cho shook his fist, his face as red as the morning sky behind him. "This money will let me start again. You don't need it," he shouted. "Your husband will take care of you."

Kimi lunged for her pack, but Cho's grip remained tight.

"Since you're a girl, I could take you as my housekeeper."

"Never."

His anger spent, Mister Cho lowered his fist and gathered his things. Hachi shook with sobs.

Mister Cho slung his packs over his shoulder, pots clanging, knives rattling. He pointed at Hachi. "Come boy. Now. We'll leave her behind."

Hachi looked at Kimi, torn.

Kimi could feel the pressure continuing to build within her. "Hachi stays with me." She reached for Cho with hands that had turned to claws. His eyes widened as he stumbled backward.

Kimi became transfixed by the sight of her hands. She blinked and they looked normal again. "What...," she mumbled, unable to continue.

Mister Cho's face turned hard. "Keep the boy. He's too little to help in the bakery." He started briskly down the road, merging into the sparse flow of early-morning refugees.

"I hope Lord Yama will find you a fitting place in Hell," Kimi shouted. "Maybe he'll send you back as a cockroach and I can step on you."

As her anger grew to rage, tingles cascaded across her brow and down her arms. Churning black clouds hung overhead. Lightening formed before it lashed out around them. A peal of thunder crashed. As large plops of rain fell on the books and the other items from her pack, runnels of pasty mud caked her dusty pants and jacket.

Hachi's screams broke through her rage.

The refugees near them had stopped and stared at her with horror. Most avoided her gaze, turning and walking away swiftly. Was she the reason for Cho to leave in such a hurry?

She crouched down so she could soothe Hachi, but he scooted back. His eyes round with terror, he stared at her hands. What had he seen? A berserker? She held her hands in front of her. They looked hazy and grey. They tingled. Bright pinprick flickers of light edged her vision.

What had she done? Mei's words came to mind. "I can see that people who were murdered would want to take over somebody else's body to wreak the vengeance that compels them. They pervert the spirit of the living person, turning them into wicked spirits." Had Grandfather or Aunt Lu turned her into a wicked spirit? No, they wouldn't do that. Besides, Kimi didn't believe in spirits. Anger had allowed evil to enter her soul.

Was Aunt Lu right? Would Kimi be sent to the Ten Hells? She shut down the thought immediately—the possibilities too painful to grasp. She shook her hands until they turned pink and lost their hazy appearance.

Everything else went back to normal, too. The rain stopped as suddenly as it had started. Kimi looked up, noting that the clouds had begun to disappear. Odd. Where had the storm come from, and how could it have gone away so fast?

Tears streaked the dust on Hachi's face. Kimi picked up an apple that had fallen from her pack and held it out to him. After he eyed her for a few moments, he grabbed it and darted away. She let him be.

She plucked the books out of the dirt, relieved to see they were undamaged. She wiped the spot of mud off the black lacquer box that held Xiao's precious gift. Xiao. Where was he?

Forget it! No time to think about him. She gathered up the rest of her scattered things. Aunt Lu's comb and mirror fell to the ground when Kimi picked up the clothes. They were her aunt's most treasured possessions. The priceless set was lacquered in black, inlaid with mother-of-pearl in a chrysanthemum pattern so precisely it had not even the tiniest gap between shell and wood. She nestled the comb and mirror into the folds of the spare pants at the bottom of her pack.

Kimi picked up the folded note her grandfather had so carefully put in the bag. Coin-sized dots of rain covered the outside of the note. She unfolded it and saw his crisp characters smudged so she could only make out half of them. The paper was as cold as Grandfather's cheek. The note was the last thing he had written, and it wasn't scholarly. It had directions to Xiao's house. She hoped she could remember enough of the blurred instructions.

Kimi checked the road behind her. No clouds of dust or other signs of a marching army. Still…she had to keep ahead of the Japanese.

She stuffed the remaining items in the pack, noticing as she did that Cho had dropped a few of the loose coins. She picked one up and put it in her pocket. She bent for another and Hachi scrambled like a little squirrel, chasing after all the other coins. When he was done he came to her, still hesitant, and dumped the coins in her palm. He moved back quickly, still showing caution. She slid the coins into her pocket to join the few already there.

Hachi's eyes went from wary to wide with dread when she lifted her restored pack onto her back.

Kimi squatted to his level and reached out to wipe his runny nose with her sleeve. "Don't worry. I'm not leaving without you," she said. "Let's go."

He didn't move.

For a moment she saw the situation from his perspective. He, too, had been betrayed. Alone. Afraid. But unlike Kimi, he had no place to go. No one would care for him except her. Perhaps Xiao would open his heart to the boy and let him stay with them.

"Hachi, we need to leave now or the Japanese will catch up to us." A moment of panic overtook her. She peered southward. Was that a cloud of dust in the far distance? The Japanese soldiers. They were miles away, but there was no more time to waste.

Trying hard to ignore body aches and pains, Kimi took several steps onto the road. When she looked back at Hachi, she was dismayed to see him standing with his fists at his side and his lips a solid line.

Kimi touched the medallion, hoping for a wagon's load of patience. She would need it. "You can come or not Hachi, but I'm not going to wait."

"What's that?" Hachi said. His finger pointed at the sky. The dark clouds were gone, and the sliver of sun peered down on them like the golden eye of a god. Something like a very large bird flew across the ridge of the hills and headed into the mountains to the north. The silhouette disappeared so fast that she wouldn't have seen it if she hadn't looked up at that exact moment. Its sinuous shape reminded her of the dragon carved into her grandfather's headboard.

"Was that a dragon, Kimi? Maybe it will come to bite off my uncle's head. Then it can come and kill all the Japanese."

Kimi didn't want to be the one to pop the bubble of his excitement. "No. Just a flock of birds. But if it were a dragon then maybe it would do just what you say."

The yellow rays of the early morning sun went behind a dense wall of clouds before disappearing into the leaden gray of the sky. Hachi came within a couple of feet of Kimi and followed her down the road.

* * *

Kimi's feeling of urgency mounted with each slow step. After an hour, she stopped and pulled a penny out of her pocket. "See this? It will buy candy once we get to the city. I will give this to you only if you hold my hand and stay with me."

Hachi looked at the coin and then at her. His glance landed on the penny once more and lingered there.

"You have to hold my hand," she repeated, keeping her voice soft, but firm.

Hachi hesitantly reached his hand toward her. Kimi handed him the money and took his small hand in hers. As they walked, waking nightmares filled her mind. Grandfather's staring eyes. Aunt Lu's crumpled body. The books and papers scattered on the floor by Grandfather's desk. The sounds of the guns and cruel laughter. The butcher dead in the street. Mei's doll-like face covered in blood. Time would never take those memories from her.

Distracting Hachi with stories of the Monkey King didn't work. Kimi was thirsty and tired and she assumed he was as well. Several enterprising farmers were selling water by the side of the road, but she couldn't use all the money on water when she still needed to buy food.

A farmhouse came into sight, nothing but a rundown mix of brick, tin, and wood stuck together without any apparent plan. An elderly woman wrapped in a brown shawl came around from the back of the stable. She carried a pail to the washtub near the road.

Kimi wiped Hachi's nose while the old woman approached in scuffling steps. She doubled her speed and smiled at them through a web of wrinkles. The woman winked before she poured the water into the tub.

"May we have some water, please?" Kimi asked.

"Of course."

"How much?"

"Nothing. The gods gave us the well and didn't charge us anything for it."

A man came around the house. "Wife, are you done with that bucket yet?"

"Almost, Husband."

He nodded at Kimi but didn't say anything to her. Instead he asked his wife, "Any dragons this morning?" he asked his wife.

"Only these travelers." The woman smiled again, her head tilted. Holding her hand against her mouth to muffle her words, she whispered to Kimi. "Years ago I saw a dragon. I saw one again today. But my husband doesn't believe me. He thinks I'm so old that I believe in children's stories."

"The only dragon you've seen, Wife, is the one hanging on the family room wall."

"Phish. I saw it in the morning sky, sure as can be. There it was, all green and gold. It seemed to be looking for someone, weaving back and forth over the road. Then in a flash it was gone." She wagged her finger at her smiling husband.

Another dragon. Maybe the farmwife saw the birds Kimi saw in the sky a short while ago.

Kimi drank until her stomach sloshed. She knew it wasn't smart, but she couldn't help herself. Hachi was just as greedy.

"My feet feel better already," Hachi announced to the woman. Caution and pain showed through his brave smile.

The woman patted Hachi's head. "It's a good thing I was here then."

"You should leave," Kimi warned the couple. "Kaisun…the Japanese are not far behind me."

"We've heard," the man said. "We'll be all right. Even the Japanese want food."

From the frown on the old woman's sun-browned face, Kimi knew his wife wasn't as certain.

The woman smiled at Hachi. "Get you gone now, young man. The day isn't getting any younger." She looked up at Kimi. "If you push, you can make it to Pianshan in another four hours."

"Thank you." Kimi bowed slightly and Hachi more deeply.

The woman smiled. "Such nice manners."

Hachi blushed then turned back toward the road.

* * *

By mid-morning the road grew crowded with refugees and farmers heading into Pianshan, each pushing forward at a frantic pace. Kimi pushed Hachi in front of her through the growing throng. The day had brightened, but the thousands of feet pounding the hard-packed dirt road had caused a dusty haze to form, obscuring much of the view ahead and behind. She couldn't tell how close the Japanese were.

Some people shouted: "The Japanese are right behind us."

"The Japanese have fallen back," others countered.

Kimi pushed forward until Hachi dragged her to a stop.

"Why do we need to go to the mountains?"

"My friend Xiao lives in the mountains. We'll be safe there. We need to get to Pianshan as fast as we can so we can get food and get across the city before the Japanese arrive. You still have the penny I gave you? You can buy several pieces of candy with that much money if we get to the market before it closes."

"I want to go back to Kaisun. I know my parents are waiting for me. Mā will be worried when she can't find me."

Kimi squatted beside him in the road, reaching out with both arms.

Stepping back Hachi crossed his arms over his chest. He stomped the dirt with his foot, claiming that small square of road. "What?"

"Hachi, your parents are dead. Your mā will be looking for you among the dead souls in the afterlife. And the longer she looks, the more hope she will have that you are safe. Perhaps the Goddess Kuan Yin will take pity on her and tell her you are alive and fleeing the Japanese." If a compassionate goddess existed at all.

"Mr. Cho said he would take me to them."

"Perhaps he wanted to get you safely out of Kaisun. Maybe he knew you would walk faster if you believed they were ahead of you."

Hachi wiped his nose with the back of a grubby hand. "Will I see my mother again?"

Taking his hands, Kimi said, "Do you know what dying means, Hachi?"

His brows scrunched up. "Is it like Mister Han's dog?"

"Yes, just like Mister Han's dog. Your mother lives with the gods now. You can burn candles for her and send her messages on prayer offerings. We are both orphans now. We have to take care of each other."

Hachi stepped into her arms and clung tightly. "I want to kill all the Japanese. I want to help the dragon."

"Perhaps someday, but right now we have to get to safety."

His little body shook with sobs, but they had to keep moving. People began racing past them, shouting as they came. Old women and young children were being loaded onto carts.

She checked the road, expecting to see Japanese soldiers marching toward her. Instead, a steady stream of desperate people fled toward Pianshan, some racing in carts, some with nothing but the clothes they were wearing.

"Are the soldiers coming?" Hachi asked.

"Yes, Hachi, the Japanese soldiers are coming."

Chapter Eleven

In most ways, their lives were harmonious. However, Tuan's travels to Pianshan caused discord.

Shi-lin feared for his safety on the road. In the years before she married, she had followed travelers on China's roads. She had seen innocents set upon by thieves, and observed cruel guards bullying the weak. More than once she had followed those evil men and dispensed justice. Dragons are not always kind and gentle.

One morning, as Tuan prepared for his monthly trip to the city, Shi-lin came to him.

"Husband, I wish to travel with you."

Tuan took her hands and in a kindly tone, said, "The road is hard and there are many dangers. I would not see you beset by vagabonds or wild beasts."

"But, Husband, those dangers may befall you as well. I would be happiest if I could share those hazards with you."

"It eases my heart to know you are here in safety."

"But I worry so."

He kissed her gently. "I shall return as soon as the ponies will carry me. We will be apart a short time only."

* * *

As the throngs of refugees became more frenzied, so did
the weather. Strands of hair whipped along Kimi's face and into
her eyes. Dust and grit swirled in cones, stinging her cheeks.
Perhaps it won't rain, she told herself. In the fall, heavy clouds
could fill the sky for days, or they could open and flood the
roads in a matter of an hour or two.

As she neared Pianshan, a dewy rain began to fall. The
sores on her feet stabbed as though her shoes had grown thorns.
Her shoulders and back burned with pain, and her nose ran.
Hachi's nose flowed so freely she had given up wiping it.

In spite of her misery, Kimi kept a steady pace. Hachi
whimpered but kept up. He stumbled on a long finger of stone
as they climbed a small hill. Rising from helping Hachi, she saw
the city of Pianshan laid out at her feet. Kimi stopped to gawk at
its enormity. It would swallow Kaisun at least four times. Tall
buildings jammed together into a solid wall of gray and brown.
Its fields stretched out like squares on a game board.

Then she looked back, hoping the Japanese had
somehow disappeared or fallen far behind. *Fàng pì!* The dust
cloud was closer. Much closer. She could see dark uniforms in
the haze.

Kimi shifted the backpack so it hung from her chest and
belly. Another traveler helped lift Hachi onto her back. The boy
held on like a tick riding a tiger's head.

She didn't know how long she could carry the double
load. Thinking about it sent tingles down her arms and up her

legs. With strength she didn't know she had, Kimi ran with an even gait past slow-moving families and around abandoned carts.

A fever of panic pushed the evacuees forward — more carts abandoned, owners shouting in terror, but she passed them all. The crowd pushed and shoved, knocking some people into the deep ditches on either side. Some crossed to the dike paths and ran towards the nearby farms. Others scattered into the shantytowns at the base of the city's outside wall. With her heart thudding, Kimi fought the urge to look behind her. What good would it do? She ran faster than she ever had in her life.

As she neared the southern gate, the Phoenix Gate, she could see the line of guards — Chinese guards — blocking the road. Refugees who were being turned away were running in panic.

Fàng pì! She had to get in. Kimi wriggled through the crowd. She nearly lost Hachi when a large man knocked into her and trampled an old woman. Kimi, swept along in the chaos, tried in vain to help the woman.

More Chinese troops poured from the Phoenix gate and formed disorganized battle lines. Even with the guards at the top of the wall, with their shiny guns pointed outward toward the Japanese, Kimi didn't see how these few dozen Chinese soldiers would succeed against the size of the approaching Japanese army.

In the confusion, a few refugees were slipping through the gate. Kimi pushed forward until she reached the guard controlling the access into the city. He was a round-faced man with a thick beard, standing proudly as though he commanded hundreds of men. Behind him two young soldiers stood at attention, looking sharp in their starched uniforms and shiny chest armor.

Hachi's weight shifted as he peered around Kimi's head. She felt his trembling body and tried to be brave.

Kimi opened her mouth to beg to be allowed inside when a large man rushed the gate. The guards knocked him to the ground, and Kimi, along with several dozen others, ran past them. Once inside, she moved quickly, knowing that the Japanese would soon attack and the Chinese soldiers would fall like mahjong tiles. Disappearing into the middle of the city had to be Kimi's best chance. The extra strength of her arms and legs slid from her. She let Hachi slide down and then shifted her pack.

Kimi looked up to get her bearings. Pianshan's buildings were taller and older than Kaisun's. The crowded streets seemed to go on forever. The people walked or ran with urgency, putting distance between themselves and the gate, refugees melding with townspeople.

Kimi held Hachi's hand and hurried toward the inner city. Though her grandfather's instructions had been ruined by the rain, she reasoned that it couldn't be too hard to cross a city and go out the other side.

Kimi followed an avenue to go north. The farther they went, the fewer people seemed panicked. They probably had no idea of the battle that would soon be raging outside.

Kimi felt like a tiny speck in this large place. Holding Hachi close, she gripped the strap of the pack with the other hand. The weight of the city's strangeness crushed her. And what an overpowering smell! Some scents were easily explained—the hot oil of something frying, the stink of fish too long from the water, the smell of rotten vegetables. But over it all lay the stench of unwashed bodies and human waste. Grandfather had once described the beauty of Pianshan. He must have seen a different part of the city.

The light dimmed when the crowded buildings to her right opened into a square surrounded on all sides by small shops. She could see an apothecary, a bakery, a butcher, and a half dozen other permanent shops. The stalls were narrow, and the late afternoon shadows made it seem as if the buildings overlooking the market leaned in toward the square. Level on level, one laundry-strung balcony above another, the apartments rose. In the center of the square, chickens and ducks squawked from crates stacked on farmers' carts. Shoppers shouted and pointed, pushed and shoved, just like the last market day in Kaisun.

Already merchants were putting away their produce. Men dragged tables into their shops as though it was any other market day. With Aunt Lu's food gone, Kimi needed to hurry or she and Hachi would go hungry. She listened to the shouted bargaining, getting a sense of the prices. Kimi felt the coins in her pocket and realized they wouldn't go very far.

Hachi cooed at a pigeon pecking at a melon rind. It flapped its wings and jumped a few feet away, eyeing its treasure jealously. Hachi stood still, one finger poking at his runny nose, and watched the bird.

Kimi wiped Hachi's nose and face with the inside of her jacket—the only part not wet and streaked with dirt. She rubbed her face with her hands, hoping she didn't look as bedraggled as she felt. Taking Hachi's hand, she approached the stalls. She wanted meat strips, dried fruit, and buns. Oh, yes, and candy for Hachi.

When Kimi reached for the coins in her pocket, she felt a prick stab her finger and her heart. She had forgotten about the piece of Aunt Lu's plate. Grief overwhelmed her thoughts. She could still see the pantry, the broken jars of peaches, and the gaping hole in the back of Aunt Lu's head.

Hachi snapped her out of the memory when he dragged her into the sweet shop. He stood first before the candy straws then moved to a jar of round candies wrapped in colorful papers.

"Hurry, Hachi. We need to buy dinner. And we have to leave Pianshan before it is completely dark."

He went back to the straws. "Can I have these?"

Kimi nodded. Hachi held out his coin to the girl behind the counter. "How many will this buy?" he asked.

The girl took his coin and pulled out four straws and then two more. "This many."

Hachi slipped them into his pocket and looked at Kimi, his face beaming.

"You strike a hard bargain, young man," the girl said.

Bowing low, Hachi said, "Thank you." Pride washed through Kimi as though the well-mannered boy belonged to her.

Kimi turned back toward the market square and made hurried purchases of meat strips, dried apricots, four apples, and a half-dozen meat buns. The buns were stale, so she bargained for a cheaper price. She gave a haughty sniff when the man gave in and wrapped them in paper. Aunt Lu would have been proud of her.

A group of women entered the market square, fear stamped on their faces. More followed. The merchants closing up brought their tables back into the market square.

"Are the bad soldiers coming?" Hachi asked.

"Soon. We need to be gone from Pianshan before then or we may be trapped here."

Kimi stopped a woman and asked directions to the north gate. She suggested they go back to the Phoenix Gate and take a path that arched around the perimeter of the city.

"I can't go straight through the middle?"

"There are other ways, but you must know the city to find them. Going through the middle is not wise."

Though the women's comments made her anxious, it would take hours to go the long way. Taking Hachi's hand, Kimi hurried from the market, taking the road that seemed to go north.

"You are going the wrong way," shouted the women.

Kimi pretended she didn't hear and kept going on aching feet. The late afternoon sun made long shadows, making the roadway between the buildings as dark as dusk. What would happen to them if she got lost? Kimi didn't even want to think about it.

Chapter Twelve

The desire to resume dragon form and soar into the skies to watch over him tormented Shi-lin. Those days alone were a trial.

To ease her loneliness, Tuan had introduced her to their neighbors, the monks at the monastery of the Mountain of Morning Song. Master Wu, the Tao Shih, head of the monastery, became her special friend. The old monk brought her books and sat with her in the evenings as she played her flute and wrote her poetry. Still, worry pulled at her and she would not be content.

Except for these monthly trips, Tuan and Shi-lin lived happily in their mountain home, firm in their love.

* * *

Kimi shivered. Their clothes were still damp from the drizzle, and a cold wind blew in gusts between the buildings. But it wasn't only the cold that drove her. It was the thought of the Japanese army forcing their way through the city's gates. At least in the city there were places to hide. But where?

Meanwhile, unkempt men leered from doorways. Feeling violated by their lewd attention, she encouraged Hachi to walk faster. Music and high-pitched laughter pushed out into the street from a hole in the wall that some might call a doorway. A dirty brown cloth was pulled to one side. Three men lounged against its folds, smoking.

One of the men leaned over to his companions and jerked his thumb in Kimi's direction. The other two laughed. The man who pointed stepped away from the wall and followed her, while the other two called out revolting suggestions.

"Hey, sweetheart," the man called at her back.

Leave us alone, she shouted in her mind.

"Are they bad men?" Hachi asked. Kimi pulled him closer and quickened their pace.

The man's steps got louder. "Spend a little time with me and my friends. We'll take good care of you and the boy. Lots of food. Warm bed." At that, the lead man's companions cheered and joined their friend, following just a few feet behind Kimi.

Prickles crawled up Kimi's back, and the familiar tingle started in her hands. Hachi ran to keep up with her. She looked over her shoulder. The men were still following with long, loping strides. They seemed to know she was boxed in and couldn't get away. She peered between doorways, seeking an alley or darkened storage room.

Kimi was tired of being afraid. She wanted to attack them, but that would put Hachi at risk. Fleeing made more sense. She pushed Hachi in front of her and told him to run as fast as he could. She ran behind him, keeping herself between him and the horrible men.

Hachi's voice came out between ragged breaths. "The men will get you...like they got my mother."

So he had seen his mother die. "If they hurt me, keep running and find a temple. They can help you. Don't worry. The drunken fools will soon give up the chase." A pain in Kimi's side threatened to take her down.

Energized by their lust, the men continued to taunt as they gained on her. This time their taunting included threats to Hachi—what they would do when they captured him.

Anger built with each of Kimi's pounding steps. More strength flowed to her arms and legs. She would not let them have Hachi.

She shouted to Hachi to keep running while she slowed, seeking a weapon. She grabbed a broom beside the doorway of a gambling hall. Holding the broom across her chest, she turned to face the men. Aicious smile crossed from ear to ear as their putrid breath engulfed her. Details of their features and clothing became sharper.

"Ahhh. The bitch thinks a little twig will protect her," said the leader. More men behind him roared, infuriating Kimi even more. They might not be Japanese soldiers but their intentions were just as cruel.

Feeling as strong as the men, maybe even a head taller, she rushed toward the drunk in the lead. She rammed his face with the broom handle, causing his nose to spray blood. The jeering laughter died, replaced by a yelp of pain. About half the men turned and ran back to the safety of their den, but more replaced them. Though their eyes were set with determination, their bodies smelled of fear.

Kimi continued forward, felling the next three men who came at her. More not-so-brave drunks ran back toward their den, screams trailing behind them. Two men still stared at her, but they kept their distance.

Kimi became aware that Hachi was a few feet behind her. She stole a glance at him. "Hachi, I told you to run!"

His eyes darted between her and the men. "It's my job to protect you. I found a safe place to hide. Come quick!"

Kimi followed him. She didn't dare waste time by looking to see if any of the men were behind her. Running as fast as six-year-old legs could carry him, he turned down an alley, then another alley, stopping at a metal staircase and the room under it. No light showed beneath the door.

"Here it is."

Hachi paused two steps into the room. Someone was bent over, ready to light a lamp on the far side of the small room. The stranger turned to face Kimi—the limited street lighting turning her face into a study of shadows. She looked no older than Kimi, yet she wore something a girl her age should never wear: a short, shape-hugging, sleeveless dress with a standup collar and three knot-buttons along a shoulder. A comb with dangling silver ornaments held up an elaborate twist of long, silky hair. The silver ornaments hung over her ear so that the shiny twisted wires jingled as she moved.

"Who are you?" the girl asked.

"We thought this room was empty."

Hachi tugged on Kimi's hand. "It was empty when I found it."

"Apologies. We need to hide from men chasing us," Kimi added.

"What are you doing in this part of town? Nice girls and little boys have no business here," she said, poking Kimi in the ribs with a shiny red fingernail. "Not the kind of business you'd like, anyway. This is the entertainment district, and unless you and your boy want to be the entertainment, we need to get you out of here."

"Do you...? Are you...?"

"Yes, yes. I am part of the entertainment. It's not the best life, especially for you." She looked Kimi up and down. "I can tell good breeding when I see it. I am Ya Niang, by the way. I have no idea why I'm getting myself into this, but Gota and his louts would have made a meal of you. I assume it was Gota — short, round, thinning hair, and the likely leader of his group?"

"The man fits your description. Thank you for helping. I'm Kimi, and this is Hachi," Kimi said, putting a protective arm across Hachi's shoulders. He shrugged her off and stood in front of Kimi, his arms crossed.

"Hachi. He's your brave defender, I see. Is he your son?"

"Oh, no. He's my friend."

Hachi looked up at Kimi and gave her a wavering smile. "She's my auntie," he said before his words were interrupted by a cough.

When he recovered he scowled at Ya Niang. Kimi hid a smile, knowing he was trying to protect her.

"It's all right, Hachi, I think she's trying to help us."

Hachi's scowl lessened, but he kept his defensive stance. He coughed again.

"Aw, poor little boy," Ya Niang said, bending down to his level. "I had a brother once." Ya Niang winced as if in pain, but the moment was gone in a blink. She stepped out of the room and returned with two cups of water. When they finished drinking she brought them more.

Kimi had never tasted anything so good. "Thank you," she said with a bow. Hachi did the same.

Ya Niang nodded and asked, "Where are you going?"

"Out of the city," was Kimi's instinctive reply.

Ya Niang laughed. "We all want that, sweetheart."

"No, you don't understand. The Japanese are probably right behind us."

Ya Niang swatted the air, as if the Japanese were of no more consequence than a fly. "Refugees? We've been seeing a lot of you in the past few days. Where are you trying to go?"

Kimi shook her head. "I'm trying to get to the north road that goes into the mountains. Grandfather told me to look for the Black Turtle Gate."

"You are a bit lost." She stuck a long fingernails into the curve of her twisted hair and scratched. "I would let you stay in my room upstairs, but someone is using it. She needed a place to lay low for a few days...you don't need to hear that story."

Done scratching, she lowered the tip of the fingernail and tapped her bright red lip.

She seemed to have made up her mind: "Damn. I have no idea what saintly spirit is taking over my brain. There's no heaven for whores that I know of. It's probably the boy. I'm a sucker for cute faces. Wait here a few minutes. Ma Dou will have what I need."

Ya Niang flipped the doorway curtain aside, sliding out with a whoosh of breath and muttered oaths. "Damn, damn, damn…" followed each of Ya Niang's footsteps up the stairs.

Why had Ya Niang become a prostitute? Certainly there must have been another choice. Or maybe there wasn't. What if Kimi's mother had been a prostitute? Did she give Kimi up so she wouldn't grow up in this life? Kimi's mind had probed that possibility before, but always dismissed it.

If she didn't have Xiao to turn to, this could have been her life. It still might be her life if she couldn't get out of Pianshan soon. Ya Niang might not be worried, but she hadn't seen what the Japanese had done.

Kimi dropped her pack and guided a sniffling Hachi to a chair. He switched his death grip from her leg to her arm, rubbing his eyes with his free hand. He needed a bed, a bath, dry clothes, and warm food. So did she. But she didn't have enough money to feed herself and Hachi if they stayed in Pianshan. Three days into the mountains, four at the most.

Ya Niang came back before they'd barely rested. She carried a bundle of clothing under her arm. Her makeup was gone and her hair was pulled back in a braid. She looked like an ordinary girl. "I'm crazy," Ya Niang muttered. "Completely out of my mind."

Kimi stood, prepared to leave. She was imposing too much. "You can just point me in the right direction. You don't need to do this for us."

"I've done stupider things. I can't stand to see people heading into deep waters on their own. Here I am, always rescuing the ones who are drowning."

That made Kimi felt a little better about accepting Ya Niang's help, but she still worried that they were putting the girl in danger.

Ya Niang dumped the pile of clothes on the table and started unbuttoning the tight silk dress.

Fàng pì! Ya Niang was entirely naked beneath the dress. Kimi turned Hachi to face the wall.

"Besides, you'll never find your way out. I don't know where you are from, girl, but even people who have always lived here get lost in this godforsaken city." She jerked a plain skirt over her hips and pulled a light blue blouse down over it. "Let's go," Ya Niang said, tying an apron around her middle. She motioned to Kimi and Hachi impatiently, and they went back into the alley while Ya Niang adjusted her clothes.

Kimi burned with frustration. She didn't like being so dependent on somebody else, but Ya Niang was right; she might never find the north gate on her own.

Ya Niang stepped in front of Kimi and Hachi, peering into the alley. "Good. Those thugs are probably inside drinking."

She hustled Kimi and Hachi out in front of her. Kimi looked back over her shoulder, half-expecting to see Japanese soldiers marching down the street. No sign of them, but the drunken men reappeared from a nearby alley.

"Celestial Gods, girl. How did you make them so angry?"

"By defending myself and Hachi. I'll do it again." Kimi pushed them back toward the hidden room. "Watch over Hachi. Don't come out until you see the men race back to their den."

Her anger rose, causing her hands to tingle as she reentered the alley. The skin on her face felt like a hard mask. The dimness of dusk fell away so she could see the fear in their eyes.

Touching the medallion for strength, she confronted the men before her.

Gota had a broomstick now, for all the good it would do him. Kimi rushed forward, grabbing his stick and breaking it like a twig. She jabbed his chest with one of the pieces. He stumbled backward with a loud crack, slumping onto the pavement and blocking the path for his friends. He didn't move when the men tried to get him standing.

Kimi tossed the stick aside and stared at Gota, at what she'd done.

One of the men checked Gota's pulse. "Stupid bitch! You killed him. I don't know who you are, but I'll tell you this—you are a dead person. Pianshan isn't big enough for you to hide."

The men seemed to lose their taste for the fight. Carrying Gota between them, they scurried down an alley.

When Ya Niang poked her head out of their hiding place, Kimi motioned for them to hurry.

"I think I might have killed Gota. We need to get out of here fast."

Ya Niang's eyes widened. "Not just fast. Very fast." She took the lead while Kimi swept up Hachi. They ran.

What had Kimi become? Had her anger made her into a monster as Aunt Lu suggested it might? Or maybe she was one of those women who performed extraordinary feats when their children were in danger. She had also heard of the kind of rage that gave men impossible strength in battle.

A hundred yards down the street, Ya Niang directed them into a narrow passage between two tall buildings that blocked the fading sunlight, making it as dark as midnight. The eyes of stray cats glowed as they wove their way between cans of overflowing garbage.

An old man huddled beside a dark doorway, barely visible. A sweet smell hung in the air around him. Kimi wasn't sure if he was even alive. Kimi longed to cover Hachi's eyes. He shouldn't see such filth or know that people could sink so low.

Ya Niang kicked the old man gently. "Don't forget the curfew, gramps. Get yourself back inside." Turning to Kimi, she said. "Opium house. Guards roust them out every so often, but they find their way back." The man slumped forward.

Hachi huddled close to Kimi's legs.

Ya Niang turned onto a wider street, more like Kaisun's. The street in front of the shops had been swept, and nothing clogged the gutters that ran down both sides of the road. The buildings were mostly brick, with brightly curtained windows above the shops.

"We can go from here," Kimi offered.

Ya Niang shook her head. "No. I'll take you all the way. Gota's men will be too distracted to bother me for a while."

"What if they turn that part of the city upside down looking for me? Will you be safe?"

"Yes. Safer now with Gota gone."

They crossed several bridges and made so many turns that Kimi knew they would never have made it through the city without Ya Niang's help. When they came to a house surrounded by a wall, Ya Niang finally stopped. The Black Turtle Gate rose over the roadway just beyond a small, tidy market square, backlit by the rising moon. Carts and tradesmen formed a winding ribbon leaving Pianshan. Apparently the Japanese weren't bothering to go past the city.

"Ya Niang," Kimi said, pleading with her eyes. "Come with us. They're letting people leave. I have a little food."

Ya Niang laughed. "And do what? Scrub floors? Harvest gourds? I'd never fit into your world. I have plans that will get me off the street soon enough. I'm learning to be a midwife. I won't need to put up with those louts anymore."

"But the Japanese are already at the southern gate. They've probably entered the city by now."

"Let them," Ya Niang said. "They'll find themselves as lost as you were." Her throaty laugh didn't seem to hold much humor. "Besides, I have no place to run. Such as it is, Pianshan is my home. Helping you might buy me a day out of Hell, but it won't be worth it if I can't pay my landlady."

Kimi felt the coins in her pocket. In helping them, Ya Niang had lost precious time from her business. "I can pay you a little. I don't have much, but we would never have made it this far without your help."

"You can't spare those coins any more than I can," Ya Niang said.

"Here," Kimi said, reaching into her pack, pulling out Aunt Lu's comb. "This will help you pay your landlady."

"Where did you get this?" Kimi heard amazement in Ya Niang's voice rather than accusation.

"It belonged to my aunt."

Ya Niang pushed the comb back at her. "I can't take this. It is a family heirloom, not something to be sold to a greedy pawnbroker. If I even get that far with it. Most likely it will be stolen. There is no private property where I live."

Nothing Kimi could say would change Ya Niang's mind. Just like Aunt Lu and Grandfather, the girl wouldn't listen to her warnings. If only she had the strength to carry every one of them to safety.

Hachi reached into his pocket and pulled out one of his candy straws and handed it to Ya Niang, punctuating his kindness with a deep cough.

"Aren't you sweet," she said, taking the candy offering and putting it in her own pocket. "Now I have been paid in full." She bowed to him, and then turned to Kimi. "You need to find shelter for a day or two. He won't make it much farther in this damp cold."

Kimi shook her head. "I have no choice. He'll be fine once we make it to the monastery at Morning Song." She hoped her words were true.

Ya Niang pointed down the road that crossed the square. "Just follow the road. It will take you under the gate. The full moon will light your path until you find a place to rest for the night."

"Thank you." Those simple words seemed inadequate.

"Well, maybe my mercy will buy me some luck tonight—someone feeling generous." The corner of Ya Niang's mouth rose, and then she turned and headed back the way they had come.

Kimi stared after her until Hachi tugged on her hand. "Are we safe now?" he asked. "Did the drunken men give up?"

"Probably not, but they won't come outside the gate for fear of not getting back inside."

"Good."

They walked another few minutes with Hachi sniffling and asking for water.

Soon the determination in Hachi's eyes melted into curiosity. "What did the Monkey King do next, Auntie?"

Then he coughed again. Deep and rattling.

Chapter Thirteen

In time, a seed of sadness grew in Shi-lin's heart. She wished to give Tuan a child. She burned prayer strips to the gods, entreating them to make her fertile, but months went by and still her moon days came.

No amount of music and meditation could quell her tears. Thick blankets of snow covered the mountains, and heavy rain fell in the valleys below.

In the month of Chrysanthemums, the goddess, Kuan Yin, came to Shi-lin as she sat weeping in her garden.

"You will bring more rain with all of your tears," the goddess said. "What troubles you?"

"I long to have a child, but my womb fails to quicken. This is a magic I do not know."

Kuan Yin smiled. "Are you certain that you wish to raise a babe? Child bearing brings trial and heartbreak even among those women who are human by birth. More than these, you would need to remain in human form, even through the pains of labor or the child will certainly die."

"Dear goddess, I am willing to accept the consequences if only there is a chance that I can present Tuan with a child of his own."

Kuan Yin agreed and told her to take a concoction of gentian, peony, and ginseng for five days after her next moon cycle. She also told her what herbs human women used to hold the baby in the womb. Shi-lin thanked the goddess with all her heart and did as the goddess instructed.

* * *

For the first time since leaving Kaisun, Kimi almost felt safe.

If Grandfather had been right, the Japanese would stay in Pianshan for a while, using it as a base before they went to the Summer Palace. Kimi doubted they'd travel this road into the mountains. For one thing, there were few farms on this route, which meant there would be little food to feed the soldiers. But then again, there had been no reason for the soldiers to massacre the people of Kaisun.

Kimi checked behind her.

The road out of Pianshan was busy, but it wasn't crowded with refugees like the road into the city had been. Some people, like her and Hachi, had their lives strapped to their backs—refugees leaving the city as a precaution. But most of the travelers seemed to be farmers and craftsmen going home without a sense of alarm. Kimi longed to shout to these people and tell them about Kaisun.

She wanted to be as far away from Pianshan as possible before they stopped for the night. But Hachi's feet dragged and hers weren't much better. With luck, a farmer would let them spend the night in his barn, but if need be they could sleep on the side of the road. Unlike the road into Pianshan, this road had no ditches and the fields were dry.

Kimi reached up and tucked a strand of hair behind her ear. She was almost willing to shave her forehead and braid her hair back in a queue like a proper Chinese man would.

Hachi squeezed her hand. "Ya Niang was a nice lady."

"Yes, she was very nice. You were kind to give her some of your candy."

Hachi shrugged. The cold gusts blew his hair into his eyes, but he had given up trying to keep it off his face. He'd given up on his runny nose, too.

His hands felt like burning coals. Kimi felt his hot, damp forehead. She had to face the fact that he was getting sicker. What could she do with nowhere to go and no money to pay for help?

When Hachi spoke his voice sounded weak. "Auntie Kimi, what did the Monkey King do next?"

She told him how Monkey and his friend Pigsy defeated the river monster and then told him other stories as well. They walked this way for an hour with Hachi's laughter interspersed with fits of coughing. His fights with imaginary monsters became less frequent.

Several times he sat in the road, unable to continue. Each time Kimi gave him a bit of the food she'd gotten in Pianshan and let him rest for a minute before encouraging him to continue. It broke her heart to see how hard he tried.

They had to find a suitable place to stop soon. Something better than the side of the road. If they had a meat bun and a few hours rest they'd both feel better. And if they were given hot tea and a warm place to sleep Kimi would think she'd gone to heaven.

After one of Hachi's coughing bouts, she couldn't persuade him to stand again. She picked him up and carried him but couldn't go more than a few hundred feet. Kimi slumped down at the side of the road holding Hachi in her lap. Desperation stole all sense of hope. She didn't know what to do.

A rough-looking man pushing a half-filled cart stopped beside them, his head too big, his hands too big. The corded muscles of his arms showed beneath the rolled-up sleeves of his frayed jacket, yet his hair was plaited in a neat queue and a pillbox hat rested properly on his head.

"My name is Wen." He pointed ahead. "The turn-off to my home is about an hour away. I could give the boy a ride that far if you want."

Hachi gave Kimi a pleading look. After Cho, she couldn't trust anyone, especially someone who looked more like a bandit than a farmer. But for Hachi's sake…

"I am Kimi, and this is…"

"Hachi," came his raspy voice.

Wen knelt so that his face was as low as Hachi's. "Are you going to be a famous general, too?"

Hachi nodded. "Just like Monkey."

Wen tousled Hachi's hair then stood and addressed his next question to Kimi. "Is he related to you?"

"He's from my town."

The farmer retrieved a pair of dried plums from his pocket. He handed one to Hachi and the other to Kimi. Hachi held the plum in his hand and looked at it for a minute, almost as if it were a puzzle he had to solve.

"Hachi, you need to eat something. It will make you feel better," Kimi said.

Hachi nibbled around its edges, and then smiled. He reached into his pocket and handed Wen one of his candy straws. "Friend," he said, which brought on another coughing bout.

"You don't feel well, do you, Hachi?" Wen said, touching his fingers to Hachi's forehead. The man's face shifted from kindness to worry. Reaching into his pocket, he handed Hachi another plum.

"This boy has a fever. Please come to my home for the night. My mother can tend to him."

Kimi looked at Hachi's glassy eyes and then at Wen. Should she trust a stranger? It wasn't as if she had a choice.

"Mother has medicine for fever. She will know how to take care of him. I have two children of my own. I would want someone to take care of them if they needed help, even if the help looked a bit disreputable."

Hachi laid his hand on Kimi's sleeve. His eyes were pinched with pain. "Auntie Kimi, can we go with the man?"

"Yes," she said, seeing no other choice.

Wen smiled and his whole face changed. He put Hachi in the cart, adjusting the small amount of food and supplies in the bottom. Kimi took off her pack and handed Wen the damp blanket. He tucked it around the little boy, picked up the handles of the cart, and started walking again. Hachi was asleep before Wen had taken twenty steps.

"You've come from the south, haven't you?"

"We're from Kaisun."

"From Kaisun? That is very far to walk for such a young boy." He shook his head.

"We had no choice after what the Japanese did. Aren't you afraid of the Japanese? They've already reached Pianshan."

"I heard rumors, but nothing official. I'm sure our Chinese bannermen will be able to keep them out. Just in case, I brought home a few extra supplies. In a few days Pianshan will welcome my cart of cabbages."

"You should take your family and hide in the mountains."

"That's not sensible. If my son and I don't harvest the cabbages we will have nothing to eat and nothing to sell."

"At least send your family away. That's what Grandfather did for me."

"My house is not easily seen from the road, and there are many places to hide nearby."

Kimi's fists clenched in desperate frustration. He wouldn't listen. Maybe his mother would understand.

They walked in near silence for a half hour. Several times the evening breeze lifted Hachi's blanket. Kimi tucked the blanket around him and stepped this way and that until she found a spot where Wen's garlic-heavy aura was fainter.

One by one the travelers that shared their road peeled off onto farm lanes until they had the road to themselves. Hachi's rattled breathing worried Kimi.

"It isn't much farther," Wen said.

Kimi's hands felt nearly frozen even with them tucked into her jacket pocket. Her concerns about Wen rose again when they turned off the road at a narrow break in a tall hedge. She'd put their lives into the hands of a rough-looking man she'd met on the side of the road. For all she knew he might not have a mother and children.

They traveled down a long, rutty lane shadowed with tall bushes on either side. Except for a thin outline of yellow light framing the door, the tiny farmhouse looked like a block of black against the charcoal gray sky. She hoped food and warmth waited for them inside.

Wen pushed the cart right up to the front of the house, then lifted a sleeping Hachi and motioned with his head for her to open the door. Following them in, she closed the door against the cold night.

The three of them were cramped into an entry no bigger than a closet. The room, much hotter than the outside air, made

Kimi sweat right away. Children's voices echoed in the background. A woman told the children to calm down, but it reduced the volume only a little.

Wen guided them to a room to the right of the entry. This room was big enough for four sleeping mats and a pot, leaving a narrow walkway to the kitchen area in the alcove beyond. Even though woven straw mats covered the walls, Kimi could still feel the cold draft that the small heater couldn't keep at bay. The purpose of the pot became clear when she looked up and saw a small hole in the roof. Someone had painted the wall mats with a mountain landscape, giving the room its one bright spot.

Two children, about six and seven, ran to Wen and tugged at his sleeves. A lean, middle-aged woman stood near the kitchen. She had thin hair pulled up in a tight bun anchored with two bamboo chopsticks. A pristine white apron covered her faded housecoat.

"Mother, I brought guests. The boy has a fever, and this young woman, Kimi, seems ready to fall from exhaustion."

The woman walked over to Kimi. "Welcome to our home. I am Biyu."

Wen tousled the hair of the children who stared at Kimi and Hachi. "These are my children," Wen said, putting his hand on the boy's head. "This is my son, Zhong and this is my daughter Jia-Li."

Zhong was heavy-set and big-boned. Jai-Li was a tiny wisp of a girl who had her grandmother's features. "Hello," they said together.

Biyu turned to the children. "Remember to be quiet, and let Kimi sleep in the morning."

"Will the boy be all right?" Zhong asked.

"Your grandmother will take good care of Hachi," Wen said. "I'm sure he'll be fine in a day or two."

A day or two? Kimi didn't have a day or two. She had to make it to the monastery before the treacherous snowfalls. But she had no choice if she wanted Hachi to recover.

Wen carried Hachi to the sleeping area and lay him on a mat near the center of the room. Biyu knelt by the boy, feeling his head with her slender hand. The lamplight illuminated her sculpted face, button nose, and high, curved brows. She looked elegant, even though the family was obviously poor.

Kimi stood at the room's entrance, not sure what to do with herself. She watched Biyu and Wen as they wrapped Hachi in a dry blanket. Though they were gentle, she expected him to wake and cry at the sight of more strangers in his life. The fact that he didn't stir sent fear through her heart.

The children watched with solemn expressions and wide eyes. After Wen had Hachi settled, he went over to them. They jumped up and circled him with their arms. He patted the boy on the head and bent to whisper in the girl's ear.

After a few minutes, Wen turned to Kimi. "Follow me. You can set your things down in here." He led her to the family room. Opposite the door, four chairs were pushed against the wall. They looked like they might have been beautiful a century ago. Now they were tired, the finish worn down to bare wood.

Kimi set her bag down and took off her coat. Going back to the bedroom, she crouched next to Hachi's mat. His lips were dry, his fever worse. Every breath seemed labored, and the gurgling in his chest never went away. He didn't move when she touched him.

Anger soured Kimi's stomach. If Hachi died it would be the fault of the Japanese. The little boy could have gotten the rest he needed if they hadn't tried to keep ahead of their army. And if Cho had carried Hachi, maybe the boy wouldn't have gotten sick. But mostly she blamed herself for not realizing how sick he was.

Wen's mother came from the kitchen and stepped over the sleeping mats to avoid spilling the bowl of water-soaked rags.

"Hachi . . . Will he be all right?" Kimi asked. She wanted to do something to help, but she had no idea what to do.

"We'll have to see," Biyu said, "but fretting will not make this little boy better. I will wake you if there is any change. You need sleep almost as much as he does." She knelt and wiped Hachi's face with the wet rags.

Kimi returned to the family room and crawled onto the mat Wen had supplied. She wanted to stay in the bedroom with Hachi, but there was no space for one more mat. She pulled the blanket over her. As she stared up at the wooden beam that ran the length of the room, she thought of all the awful things that had happened. She longed for Aunt Lu to hold her, to hear Grandfather breathe a word of praise. A lone tear crawled down her cheek. Hugging the blanket to her she drifted off to sleep.

* * *

In her dream, Kimi sat on the garden bench in Kaisun and watched the carp as they lazily swam to and fro in the pond. Someone sat next to her, and she jumped to her feet, her heart pounding. She took hurried steps away, backing to the edge of the pond. It was the old woman she'd met while walking on the road north before Cho had stolen their money — the woman with the faded finery and wise manner.

Kimi released the breath she'd been holding.

"Come, Tengshe. You have nothing to fear from me," the woman said, motioning for Kimi to return to the bench.

Kimi relaxed and sat beside her. Who was this woman? Where did she come from?

"If you aren't careful with your tears, you will flood all of China." The old woman's eyes seemed to laugh as though she had said something witty. Drops of water from the tips of rain-soaked leaves fell into the pond. The orange and white snouts of the carp nosed up, biting at the drops on the surface.

"Your tears won't bring back the dead, you know," the woman continued, looking sad.

"No, I suppose they won't." Kimi looked at her own hands folded in her lap. She'd lost so much—family, home, hopes for the future. She had so little left—Hachi, a few treasures, honor, and pride. And those weren't certain. But what could she do?

She watched the carp for a few more minutes. Who would take care of them? Several leaves had blocked the spillway that led to the carp pond. Kimi got up and cleared the channel then went back to sit beside the old woman.

What an odd dream. Her dreams never had this much detail.

"Not all dreams are dreams, you know."

Kimi tried to make sense of the comment but couldn't.

"How goes your journey?"

"Not well. Hachi is sick, and I shouldn't take him into the mountains with me. He might even die. I wish I could get word to Xiao. He could come get us when Hachi's well again."

"Are you sure you want to go to Xiao? Have you forgiven him?"

"For leaving town before the Japanese came? For not helping me get Grandfather and Aunt Lu to safety. Or for quitting his position at Court to go plant potatoes?"

Kimi knew she wasn't being entirely fair about Xiao, but she felt too angry to hide the truth. She hadn't thought much about his offer to release her from the marriage contract—too many things had happened. But now it seemed like no choice at all. If she didn't marry Xiao, what else would she do? Maybe she could change his mind about living in the mountains. It was her only hope of having the future she'd dreamed of.

"There are always choices," the woman said, as though she could read Kimi's thoughts.

None of them very good. "You mean I could be like Ya Niang? Be a prostitute? What would happen to Hachi if I did that?"

"There may be better choices."

Kimi shook her head again, not sure what the old woman meant.

"You should not blame Xiao. He could not have known." The woman's words were spoken gently, but to Kimi they sounded like scolding. But he had not been there when she needed him, and he might not be there now.

"Whatever you do, marry Xiao or leave him forever, it won't be an easy decision. You are an extraordinary child to have come this far on so little. Take care, Tengshe." The woman paused, her eyes filled with sadness. Then she stood and walked into the garden as a mist gathered about her. She followed the path where it turned behind the pine tree and disappeared. Kimi gasped and rose to chase after her, but the woman had disappeared. Not even a tendril of mist remained.

Chapter Fourteen

Before three months had passed and the crocuses had just reached tiny arms above the snow, Shi-lin was certain that she was pregnant.

As they sat in the garden one day, watching the afternoon shadows fall toward evening, Shi-lin spoke to Tuan.

"There is news I must share with you."

He smiled. "What news is that?"

"The greatest news a wife could ever give her husband. I am with child."

Tuan took her hands. "How can this be? I did not expect children. Our natures are too different. Is this a special magic?"

She could tell he was proud, delighted, and concerned all in the same moment. The warring thoughts were on his face and in his voice.

"It is no magic, at least none of my doing. I have become pregnant in the manner of human women, and I will deliver this child in that manner as well. Whether the babe will possess magic, I cannot tell."

He looked worried.

"Are you not happy, Husband?"

His face changed such that the morning sun had never beamed so brightly. "Beyond joy, my love. It is only that I worry for you. Perhaps I should stay with you and let one of the monks carry my chests to the market at Pianshan."

"That is not necessary. Master Wu will see to my needs. All will be well." These were the words of her mouth but the words of her heart wished she could travel with him to protect him.

* * *

When Kimi woke, she blinked several times before she recalled where she was.

Hachi. Was he all right?

She tiptoed into the room where Wen's mother lay curled up beside the swaddled boy.

Kimi stepped around the out-flung arms and wayward feet of the sleeping family until she was looking down on Hachi's face. She gently touched his forehead. Even before her fingers reached his skin, she could feel the heat. She touched the medallion wishing it could somehow heal the boy. When he breathed in and out, she could hear throaty gurgling at the end of each breath. Even her grandfather's breathing had not sounded so bad.

The bowl of damp rags lay at Biyu's feet. Kimi took a rag and knelt at the end of the bed to wipe the little face, wishing she had the power to do more for him. He might have died if not for the kindness of Wen and Biyu. He might still die. The thought struck terror into her heart.

A short time later Biyu rose, motioning Kimi to stay put. Kimi listened to the clatter of pans and dishes as Biyu made the family's breakfast. The children got up to help their grandmother set the table, and Wen brought Kimi a bowl of oatmeal. The unity of the family scene made her miss Grandfather and Aunt Lu even more. If she could forgive Xiao, maybe she could have a family like this.

Once the family had eaten their breakfast, Wen carried Hachi into the family room where Biyu could keep an eye on him while she worked at her embroidery. Such beautiful work Biyu did. This piece had red, green, and blue dragons on the borders of a man's black robe. Her fingers flew unerringly in and out of the fabric without her seeming to watch. Her hands paused to change threads so quickly Kimi's eyes could hardly follow. And while Biyu sewed, she spoke, her hands keeping the rhythm of her words. She told fables—one after another. Jia-Li handed her grandmother bobbins of silk thread when needed. The words were like a soothing song. Kimi might not believe the stories themselves, but the words and familiar cadences had their own magic. Her shoulders relaxed a bit.

Kimi continued to bathe Hachi's face throughout the day. He slept fitfully, hardly ever waking, even when coughs shook his little body. When he did, she had him drink the herbed infusion Biyu had made.

As the hours wore on, Hachi's breathing worsened. The rattle in his chest was continuous now, and his breath came in short gasps. At noon, Biyu set down her work and bent over Hachi. "I don't like his breathing," she commented.

"Is there anything I can do?"

"Hold him up and rub his back for a few minutes. I will do something my grandmother taught me."

Biyu made a tent over Hachi. "This will hold the steam in," she explained as she left the room.

Kimi could hear Biyu moving in the kitchen. She came back carrying the tea warmer. She set it on the floor in the opening of the tent. Then she brought in a small pot of steaming water.

Jai-Li and Zhong stood side-by-side watching. When the steam started to flow in the tent, the children squatted and began asking questions, one following the other in a burst of youthful curiosity. They wanted to know everything about Kimi's life.

"What was your house like?"

"What colors were your fish?"

"How big is Kaisun?"

"How many people died?"

"What was your grandfather like?"

"Was he strict with you?"

She answered all their questions except the ones about what happened in Kaisun. This is all she said: "The Japanese soldiers came. Many people died, including Hachi's parents, Grandfather and Aunt Lu. We left in a hurry and came here."

Eventually, Biyu declared an end to the questions and sent the two outside. Kimi decided to try and reason with her.

"Biyu, on our way here I mentioned to Wen that it would be safest if your family went away into the mountains for a while to be safe from the Japanese. You cannot imagine the devastation in Kaisun. Very few people escaped. I hid, but I was lucky. Wen doesn't seem willing to leave."

The lines around Biyu's eyes deepened. "His life is here, Kimi. He needs his farm to survive. Besides, the handcart could not carry the children; it can barely carry the food, blankets, and spare clothing we'd need. They would have to walk, and Hachi cannot do that now. Wen thinks he can protect his children better here than on the mountain road."

"Are you sure he won't change his mind? Perhaps you could stay at the monastery on the Mountain of the Morning Song."

"We'd likely be snowed in until after planting time. Is that where you are going? Wen said you are traveling to your husband's house. Perhaps I know him."

Kimi shook her head. "He is not my husband yet. His name is Long Xiao. My grandfather told me to go to him. Xiao lives on the mountains a day beyond the monastery, but I don't think he's lived there very long."

Biyu's mouth formed a perfect circle. "That's three or four days at least. Good thing Wen found you. Hachi wouldn't have survived the journey. So his family is dead? You're sure of it?"

Kimi nodded.

They sat for a few more minutes, listening to Hachi's rough breathing.

"How do you know Xiao?" Biyu asked. "He lives so far from Kaisun."

"He lived with us for a while when I was young." Kimi lowered her gaze, trying to discourage any more questions about Xiao.

"You don't want to marry him, do you?" Biyu said.

Kimi realized her doubts had shown through "I don't know. I don't think so."

"Why ever not? I can't imagine a kind grandfather would agree to a marriage contract with a beast."

Kimi looked down at her hands. "No. Xiao's not a beast. He had a promising career at the Empress's Court, and he gave it up to be a farmer." How rude that sounded! Biyu and Wen were farmers. "I didn't mean . . ."

Biyu laughed. "Don't fret yourself. If I had a chance to live at Court, I wouldn't be content with the idea of being a farmer's wife, either."

Kimi realized how petty her complaints sounded now. Staying alive, having enough to eat, not living on the street as Ya Niang did—these were the things that really mattered.

"I understand," Biyu said. "You want to make your own decisions. You think it isn't fair."

These words surprised Kimi. Biyu did understand.

"But you are young. Soon you will realize that your elders know what is best for you. You will find happiness with your husband, keeping his house, raising his children. It has been this way for thousands of years because it is the proper way. You will see. Then when your daughter comes to you, unhappy about the marriage contract, you will tell her the same thing. We do this because it is right."

But it wasn't right. Most women didn't have a say, and a thousand years hadn't made it right. It was a new world now.

"What about you? Did you know your husband before you were married?" Kimi asked.

Biyu's stared into the distance, her eyes softening. "Our fathers were friends from the market. They were like brothers. They decided we would marry when we were both still very young. We lived far from the city. I never met him, though from the stories my father shared, it felt as though I already knew him."

"When did he die?"

"Oh, many years ago. Wen was not much more than a boy—at least I thought so. He became a man very fast. Wen and his wife worked the fields together. Even with his wife's death Wen has, bit-by-bit, brought the farm back to where it used to be before his father died."

"Does Wen miss his wife?"

She nodded. "He loved her very much. They were going to have another baby, but it came early. Both his wife and the baby boy died."

So much death. So much loss. "Do Zhong and Jia-Li remember their mother?"

"Zhong does a little, though he prattles on about her as if he knew her well. That's because Wen tells him stories about her."

Kimi wished she had memories of her mother. Any memories.

Biyu set her mouth in a playful grimace. "Zhong believes his mother was a goddess. His future wife will not compare well, I fear."

"Let me fix lunch," Kimi said, patting Biyu on the knee. "We'll talk again later."

* * *

On the second day, Hachi's breathing showed no improvement, and his fever had not come down. On the morning of the third day, his fever broke. He even sipped water from a cup.

Just when Kimi thought he would get better, a vicious, wracking cough settled in. By nighttime the fever had returned.

During the day a friend of Wen's came and shared the news that the Japanese had breached the city walls and were controlling access in and out of Pianshan, but it seemed they were letting farmers through. Kimi knew that Wen's family was running short of food, so she wasn't surprised when Wen announced that he was going to go to the city. He and Biyu talked quietly for a few minutes. Biyu sounded frightened. Still, Wen departed after he loaded his cart.

The hours grew long as they waited. Zhong and his sister played quietly in the corner without speaking. Biyu pricked her finger with her sewing needle. Kimi tended Hachi. After several hours, she heard footsteps.

It had been dark for hours when Wen returned. After he ate the meal Biyu placed before him, he described what happened in Pianshan. The Japanese guards at the gate had waved him in and Wen had been able to sell his crops in the market. He said he felt their eyes on his back the whole time, and when he tried to leave the city with his cart partially loaded with foodstuffs, the Japanese guards at the gate stopped him, claiming half the food as a tax before letting him go.

That piece of news frightened Kimi. How long would it take until the Japanese came through the countryside looking for food? And what would Wen's family do for food if the soldiers came to their house? Once more Kimi tried to convince Wen to take his family and go into the mountains. And once more Wen explained why he couldn't afford to do that.

The pattern of Hachi's fever breaking each morning only to return in the evening continued. After several days, it was clear Hachi wasn't making any progress. He was weak and taking little food or water. Even the attentions of Zhong and Jia-Li couldn't rouse him for long.

Biyu said he needed an expensive medicine. Wen decided to try taking another load of cabbages to the city and to purchase the medicine with the proceeds. Kimi knew that Wen needed the money to buy food for his family, but she didn't say anything. Without the medicine, Hachi might die.

The next day Wen loaded his cart and left for the city. Within a few hours he returned, his cart still full of cabbages. When Biyu asked what happened, Wen shared that as he got halfway to the city he met several farmers returning without their carts. They warned him not to go, that the Japanese were confiscating all food, all carts, and all animals.

Biyu tried to assure Kimi that Hachi would get well even without the medicine, but it would take longer. Kimi looked at how thin Hachi had grown and wished she could believe her.

Biyu stopped her embroidery later that afternoon and came to sit by Kimi, who was mending some of the family's clothing. Her stitches weren't as deft as Biyu's, but they were good enough to mend clothes.

The set of Biyu's eyes was firm like Aunt Lu's when about to say something she knew Kimi didn't want to hear. "Kimi. Don't fool yourself. Your Hachi isn't going to be well enough to travel with you for weeks. By then the mountain roads will be impassable. Go to your Xiao, and return in the spring. Don't worry about the boy. My son won't say so, but he is quite taken by him. If you don't return to us, Wen will raise Hachi like the son he lost when his wife died. He will soon find a way to get that medicine."

"But you need the money for food, especially if Wen won't be able to sell his cabbages."

"Don't you worry about that. We've had lean years before, and we'll have them again."

This got Kimi thinking that this family's times would be leaner if she remained as another mouth to feed. She should be glad they would keep Hachi, but how could she let the child down after he'd already lost so much? How could she abandon him too?

But she had nothing to offer him. Nothing, unless Xiao was willing to take the boy in—as a son, not a servant. Touching the pendant, Kimi longed for a connection with her mother. Had her mother felt this way? Is that why she had left her with Grandfather?

"It is you I'm worried about." Biyu continued. "The mountains are dangerous any time of the year, but especially now. Snow and ice can come without warning, even this early. Wild animals are looking for their last good meals before winter. You are welcome to stay with us until spring. Your Xiao will wait." Biyu's eyes looked hopeful. "It would be good to have another woman in the house again."

Kimi was touched by the generous offer. Staying would be safest. She could put off seeing Xiao for another few months. Maybe by then she would feel better about being his wife. But as tempting as it was, she couldn't accept their hospitality.

"Thank you. I know you'll take good care of Hachi. But I can't stay. I have to keep going. I'll try to come back before the roads close and bring the medicine Hachi needs."

"Well, think about it. We'll talk about it again in the morning."

* * *

Kimi tossed and turned all night, waking several times. The best way to help Hachi get better would be to find Xiao and come back with medicine and a cart to take the boy with them. But perhaps she was being selfish in wanting to keep the boy with her. Wen had a loving family. Hachi would have a grandmother and a brother and sister.

But what if the Japanese came? There was little she could do to protect the family and Wen couldn't do better. If only there were a way to take Hachi with her into the mountains now...

As she was hanging laundry later in the morning, she saw a flock of cranes pass overhead. No black one. But as she watched, envying their freedom, one of the cranes split away from the formation and headed toward the mountains. She draped the last work shirt over the line and watched as the bird continued his solo flight.

Yes, that was her, leaving her flock. Kimi had never felt so alone. But the bird was not trapped. It chose its own path. Up to now her choices had been governed by others. The next choice was hers. She could go or she could stay.

As for going to Xiao, Biyu was right; he wasn't a beast. He was stubborn and aloof, but not cruel. And she didn't have to be ruled by him. She would be an equal partner in the relationship. Not many women were given the choice Xiao had given her to end the contract if she wished. If she could convince him to come down off his mountain when it got safe, there would still be hope for her future.

Kimi had the power to choose. She could stay with Wen's family through the winter or go into the mountains. Traveling alone would be risky, a risk she didn't mind taking. Leaving now would be the best thing she could do for Hachi. And in going to Xiao, she would be honoring her grandfather's wishes. But Grandfather and Biyu weren't making this choice. It was her decision, and hers alone.

* * *

Kimi sat by Hachi before dawn the next morning, her bag already packed. Hachi, still listless from the fever, tugged at Kimi's jacket

Worry showed through fever-bright eyes. "Don't go, Auntie Kimi. There are wild boars and tigers."

His plaintive voice stabbed Kimi's heart. Once more, she had to remind herself why she had to leave. If her plan to return with medicine worked, Hachi would get well and she could take him far away from Pianshan and the Japanese.

She bent down to be eye-to-eye with Hachi. She wouldn't lie to him like Mister Cho had, but she didn't want to raise expectations either. "I must go. I promised Grandfather I would find Xiao. It's a matter of honor. And I will bring medicine back for you as soon as I can."

"But what about the tigers?"

"I outran the Japanese, didn't I? I'll be safe."

Hachi didn't say any more, but his unhappiness showed in the worry lines on his small forehead.

"Grandmother Biyu will take good care of you. Zhong and Jia-Li will play with you. All will be well." She hoped her words were true.

Kimi shivered as the family assembled in the frost-covered courtyard. Biyu came from the house a few minutes later, carrying a square satchel with a flap that folded over the top.

"This is too much food," Kimi protested when she lifted the flap. While there were a couple of rolls, most of the bag had been filled with long strips of pork, fistfuls of nuts and dried fruit—food that would last, things that Wen's family needed for winter.

"You will be hungry, and there are few places to stop."

"Auntie Kimi?" Hachi stood just inside the front door on wobbly legs.

Kimi reached the entry before the others. "It's okay, Biyu. I'll put him back to bed. I have an idea that might help us say goodbye for now." She bent and picked up two nearly identical rocks and held them up for the others to see. "Special rocks."

Wen looked puzzled. Biyu nodded. "I see," she said with a wink.

Kimi escorted Hachi back to his bed, shrugged off her packs, and sat beside him.

"Auntie Kimi! Auntie Kimi! Don't leave me!"

She held him close to her chest, letting their tears mingle. "Oh, Hachi. I have to go, and you have to stay until you get well. I'll miss you so much. Every day. I have a surprise. I found these special rocks near the steps. Do you see what makes them special?" She held the rocks up and pointed to a white swirl in each one.

Hachi looked puzzled but nodded.

"You take my rock, and I'll keep your rock." She handed one of the stones to Hachi. "Here," she said, "you put your hands around this rock and I'll put my hands around the other rock. Each of us will squeeze very hard. Ready?"

After a minute Kimi handed her rock to Hachi and he handed his to her. "See, Hachi? We each have our own special rock. You keep mine in a safe place, and I'll keep yours until I see you again. I don't know when that will be, but someday I will find you."

Hachi looked more hopeful.

"Will you rest and get well again for me?"

He nodded.

She gave him another hug. "Wait here, Hachi. I will be right back. I have to use the washroom."

Kimi kept Biyu's bag with her and went to the kitchen door and unpacked most of the food. Then she went to the washroom and let the door slam shut.

Hachi had already fallen asleep by the time she returned, clutching his rock tight to his chest. Kimi went back to the courtyard. Turning to Wen's children she said, "Hachi is asleep. I gave him a special rock. Please be sure he doesn't lose it."

They nodded, looking at her with gentle eyes.

She bowed to Wen. "You've been so good to us. I'll never forget. I'll ask my ancestors to protect you." She didn't think the ancestors would stop the Japanese, but Wen and Biyu would value her offer.

Wen and Biyu bowed, and with a gentle nudge so did Zhong and Jia-Li.

Kimi lifted both packs and slung them over her shoulders. She closed her eyes for a moment then turned onto the path. Reaching the end of the lane, she checked for signs of the Japanese army. There were no crushed bushes, trampled undergrowth, or scuffed-up roadway. Without looking back, she began her long walk to the mountains.

Chapter Fifteen

As the summer fled and her belly grew, Shi-lin's joy grew with it, each day more certain that the child would be brought full term.

Shi-lin practiced meditation, played happy music, and ate only things that came from earth, briar, and tree. Neither did she use any strong seasonings, but followed the simple diet of the monks.

Tuan doted on her, taking her chores and insisting she stay at the monastery when he was away. Each time he returned joy danced in her heart anew. Every step they took on the path to his home was a declaration of their rekindled love.

On a glorious autumn day Tuan returned early from Pianshan. A crisp breeze carried golden leaves through blue skies. He found Shi-lin in the monastery's library writing in her book of poetry where she recorded these happy months, anticipating Tuan's child.

When she heard his familiar step she rose quickly and turned to him, crossing her arms against her chest to contain the joy inside her.

He took her into the garden and presented her with a black lacquered box inlaid with a blue dragon on the lid. The box was a treasure in itself, but Tuan bade her to open it. Lying in the crimson silk was a medallion of purest silver. It was a finely wrought dragon curving around a silvery blue pearl that was held in its claws. A silken cord passed cleverly through the dragon's mouth.

She touched it tenderly with a finger. "I am without words," she said, and a single tear touched the pearl in the dragon's belly.

He lifted the token of his love and settled the cord around her neck. She treasured the gift and wore it next to heart.

Shi-lin treasured the gift, but having Tuan in her arms was even more precious. Such was their joy that no gray thoughts clouded their happiness.

* * *

The month of the Chrysanthemums returned, and Tuan settled Shi-lin into the monastery and made his last journey to the city. The snows were due, and the baby was expected soon after. He would return with the midwife and all the things Shi-lin would need for the child's first months.

But two weeks went by, and he did not return. Master Wu tried to ease her heart. Surely the midwife had been delayed, and they would soon arrive. Shi-lin wanted to fly to Tuan and see him safely home, but the baby was part of her now, and she could not abandon it so easily.

Another week went by, and he still did not return. Nothing Master Wu said could keep her from despair.

The goddess, Kuan Yin, came to Shi-lin early one morning as she sat alone in the monastery courtyard.

"Dear child, what sadness darkens your spirit?"

"Tuan has not returned. I fear he has been harmed." Tears came to Shi-lin's eyes. "If he does not come soon the snow will lie so thickly that he will not be able to cross the mountains. Perhaps he is already caught in a drift and freezing. If I go to him maybe I can save him. I must take dragon form and search for him, but I cannot risk losing our child."

Shi-lin began to sob. "He is my life and soul. I must find him."

Kuan Yin touched her lightly. "Hush, child. Your tears are bringing even more snow. It is beyond my power to protect the babe should you change. I promise to send heavenly messengers to search for him. You tend to the child. She will need you."

"A girl? It will be a girl?" Shi-lin felt a brief moment of joy despite her worry. She would have a daughter to brighten her days.

Shi-lin thanked the goddess and prayed to Tuan's ancestors that he be found.

* * *

The day dawned clear. Warmed by the sun, Kimi frequently reached out to grab a little hand no longer there. With each mile between her and Hachi, the painful loss stretched—a band ready to break. Though she didn't want to admit it to herself, her journey was easier without having Hachi to slow her down. She told herself Monkey stories as she walked to ease the pain caused by his absence.

The road was smooth at first and free of travelers. By midday, ruts ran in narrow tracks where carts had been pulled through mud. Rocks protruded from the soil in the fields next to the road, earth's bones refusing their earthy cloak.

Kimi pushed forward. Her legs were heavy, her feet sore. The straps dug into her shoulders and pulled on her muscles. Passing each farm that afternoon, she resisted the urge to stop and ask for shelter. She had to keep going as long as she could.

Between the farms, birch trees clung tenaciously to the scant soil around tumbles of large boulders. Autumn leaves topped the white trunks, so intensely red that the trees almost looked as if on fire. That meant freezing nights. She picked up her pace. Wen had said three nights. She needed to do it in two.

Late in the afternoon the farms became farther apart. The few small farms she saw were in the forested valleys between ridges where the wind and rains had exposed the bare rock beneath. They were even poorer than Wen's farm.

The road climbed, winding along the mountain range's rocky roots. Walking became harder. After each crest, the road dropped steeply down again. At the top of each ridge she looked back, making sure there were no Japanese on the road behind her. Apparently her grandfather had been right; they had no reason to be following this road.

As the day progressed to evening, the rising spots in the road outnumbered the places where the road descended. A biting breeze made her cheeks tingle. Her legs strained on the climbs, and her thighs stretched painfully when walking down. Still, the road had no travelers or animals. The forest and hills were spectacular in their fall colors, but so isolated, so lonely.

Kimi sang children's songs, then laughed at her folly. She was heading somewhere she might not want to go, to marry a man she might not love, to plant potatoes. And he might not even be there.

More rocks. More hills. More time to think.

Her hopes rested on convincing Xiao to move to a city, if the Japanese hadn't destroyed them all. They would have a steady income, and he would be given the respect of a high scholar. Kimi would be able to start her school. With plenty of money they could afford to keep Hachi. Xiao could train him to be a scholar. In a city she could have babies with midwives and doctors. A pretty dream, far-fetched, but pretty. What made her think he would listen to her now any more than he had in Kaisun?

For the next hour, she walked with her head down, lost in her thoughts, not seeing much except the road a few feet in front of her. When she woke to her surroundings, the sun was almost gone, the forest cold.

When she finally stopped, the bags thudded as she let them slide off her back. The gourd that carried her water was almost empty, but she drank it all anyway. Dizziness almost overtook her, so she reached into Biyu's satchel for a couple of pieces of dried fruit. She nibbled them, letting the sweetness fill her mouth. Little by little her energy returned. She began to notice the small noises of the wilderness—birds calling, the scratching, scrambling sounds of squirrels—some sounds unexplained.

She picked up her packs and started up the road at a quick pace, eager to get as far as she could before the sun finally set.

Darkness arrived in the forest. It was as though she blinked and someone blew out a candle. She could still see the grey shapes around her, but even that much would be gone soon.

Fàng pì! Kimi didn't want to stop just yet. She thought of the medicine Hachi so desperately needed, but the dense weave of branches and leaves blocking the moon left her no choice. Too dark to keep going. If she fell and broke a bone, she would die, and Hachi would think she'd abandoned him.

In the dim light she looked around to find a safe place to sleep—a place that wasn't an animal's lair. Then she saw the outline of a small log cabin sheltered beneath a large oak tree just off the road. It was no bigger than her garden shed in Kaisun. A blanket of leaves covered the ground like a quilt of scraps, right up to the door. It looked as though no one had been there recently. Even so, she walked partway around the hut to see if a donkey or cart had been pulled up out of sight.

She called out to be sure. No answer. Just a rustle of leaves. She tried the door cautiously. Cracked and warped, it scraped when it opened. It became clear the cabin was deserted.

A hole in the roof had let in leaves that covered a wide bed platform built against one wall. A stone fireplace with charred logs filled the opposite wall, a small woodpile stacked next to it. Leaves splattered the hearth in uneven patches. There was nothing else but open floor and bare walls—not even a window. Through chinks in the logs she could see the clearing around the hut.

Kimi shimmied out of her pack and set it on the platform. She looked at the fireplace longingly, but it would be foolish to expose her location with a stream of smoke. She shivered, thinking of the dark, cold night ahead of her. Against her better judgment, she piled a few logs in the center of the fireplace. Using a piece of flint and some dried leaves, she lit a small fire.

She sat on the platform and ate just enough to take the edge off her hunger, then made a pillow of fallen leaves and lay down on the platform. She looked through the gap in the roof. If there were stars sprinkling the night sky, she couldn't see them. She missed Hachi, she missed Aunt Lu and Grandfather, she even missed Xiao. But her aloneness didn't feel empty. Somewhere out there Japanese soldiers were killing Chinese villagers, and nearby there were wild animals and things unseen. Kimi didn't want to close her eyes in this strange place, but the warmth of the fire made her sleepy. Soon her eyes grew so heavy she could not keep them open.

Kimi jerked awake when twigs snapped outside. Men's voices sounded close. Her mouth went dry. The fire had died down, but the room seemed lighter even though morning was still a long way off. How was it possible that she could see things that had been shrouded in darkness earlier?

The door opened, and a shaggy-headed man came through holding a knife that curved up wickedly to the tip. His gaze settled on Kimi, his features morphing into a lewd sneer. A smaller, younger, even shaggier man followed him into the room. The younger man's eyes were shaped oddly, and he had the vague stare and jerky movements of a simpleton.

Kimi's thoughts froze. Scooting back against the cabin wall, she pulled her blanket up under her chin as though that would somehow offer protection.

"Look what we have here, Paju," the first man said in a menacing voice. "We have caught ourselves a little bird." A spark glittered in his shadowed eyes.

A streak of fear fizzed through Kimi, filling her with dread.

The first man slid the gruesome weapon into the sash around his waist. Unruly hair trailed down the sides of his face, and a patchy beard covered his chin, making him look like a wild goat. The men even smelled like wild animals.

Kimi wanted to become a mouse and disappear through one of the gaps in the wall.

The bigger man stopped in the middle of the room, his hands on his hips, a hand inches from his belt knife. His gaze rested on Kimi. His smile turned up cruelly, showing his blackened teeth.

She tried to push farther back, wishing the rotten logs in the wall would give way so she could escape. The cold, rough logs pressed against her spine.

Biyu had given her a knife to slice the pork. Kimi reached down to grab her bag off the floor. The larger man jerked it out of her hands.

"What do you have in there, little bird?" he asked, opening the sack and pouring its contents onto the floor. He squatted, tucking his loose hair behind his ear, lifting Biyu's little knife between two fingers. He held it out in front of him. His eyes looked red in the reflected light of the fire.

"Think you can kill me with this, little bird?" he asked, raising the paring knife for his brother to see.

"Kailì, her knife is so little. It's a baby knife." Paju giggled, high and senseless.

Kailì continued pawing through her possessions. He shoved the books aside, sending them spinning across the floor towards the fire.

Her face flamed with humiliation when he started unwrapping the bundle of her moon day cloths. He seemed to know what he'd found because he tilted his head up to look at her with a knowing sort of sneer. No amount of washing would remove the taint of his touch on her most private things.

He thumbed through the folded cloths. Picking up her aunt's mirror and comb, he gave them a careless toss. Kimi watched with sick dread as the mirror fell in a slow arc to the hard-packed dirt floor, knowing it would break. The glass burst from the frame in glittering splinters, and the backing cracked into two pieces. A piece of the mother-of-pearl inlay spun away. The comb bounced twice and landed near the wall between the door and the fireplace. She should have made Ya Niang take them. Better that than to watch them destroyed.

"No," she cried out and scrambled to the edge of the platform, intending to go after the comb. When Kailì looked at her with malice, she slid back into her corner.

He grabbed her outer coat from the end of the platform and felt the pockets. He found nothing but the shard of her aunt's plate. He dropped it to the floor beside the platform. "You keep strange treasures, little magpie."

He handed the coat to the younger man. "Here, Paju. See if it fits."

Paju scrambled past the larger man to snatch at the shiny black box peeking out from under her spilled clothes. His oddly slanted eyes narrowed as he retreated to the fireplace and held the box in his greedy hands. Kailì turned and reached out a hand. Paju jerked the box back and said, "Mine."

"I just want to open it for you so you can see what's inside."

Paju's finger brushed over the inlaid dragon on the top of the box. He cautiously, and ever so slowly, held the box out for his brother's help.

Kailì undid the latch and lifted the white jade crane by the red silk cord. Paju's eyes followed, his mouth pinching to a perfect roundness. The fire's light made the translucent jade glow reddish orange. Kimi knew it was a crane, but for a moment it looked like a dragon in flight. With gentle hands, Paju set the black lacquered box onto the hearth and cautiously reached for the silk cord as though it were a sacred artifact.

Kailì went back to sorting through Kimi's things, letting out a triumphant snort. "Ah, here's what I wanted. I thought I heard the music of coins." He held in his hand the small amount of change left from the market in Pianshan. The man frowned, though, when he pushed the coins around in his palm and saw there weren't many. He looked up at her, "Why, you're almost as poor as we are, little bird. Where did you steal that fancy crane and these things?" he asked, picking up the comb and pointing to the splintered mirror. "Take these from your landlady?"

Paju cried out, then started sobbing, "I didn't mean to. Pretty birdie." In his cupped hand he had the body of the crane, white and lifeless, while the head still dangled from the red silk cord. The fire shone red through the severed head.

Kimi put her hand over her mouth to keep from crying out. Xiao's precious bird. Her aunt's favorite mirror. Was Paju going to destroy everything she had left?

While Paju sobbed, his brother, Kailì, came and sat at the end of the bed, so close he could have touched her. She tried to bunch up even more, but she was already wedged in the corner as far she could go. The man reached out with his hand toward Kimi. "And what are you worth, little bird? I'm sure someone will pay to see your pretty face, yes?" The look of greed in the man's face shattered any hope that he would let her go. "I wonder what brings you into the woods. Little bird has flown her cage. Who is coming to meet you here? A lover, perhaps?"

He touched her cheek, pretending to caress it lovingly. Nothing tender about the hungry look in his eyes or the way his lips parted. She turned her head away from his hand and pushed him away.

Cold beads of sweat formed on her forehead. Weak with fear, Kimi fought the urge to cover her head with her arms, not wanting him to see her fear.

He pushed his hand hard between her knees and grabbed her in a place only a husband should touch. Anger, shame, and cringing fear exploded like fireworks. Her vision dimmed, and she heard ringing in her ears. She whimpered.

"Well, for now, you are mine."

Helpless tears flowed, but a seed of hate had been sown.

"Later I'll have such sweet dreams," he said, grabbing his crotch. "But I want to be warm when I dream. Paju, go get some firewood and build up the fire."

"The birdie's dead, Kailì. The birdie's dead," Paju sobbed, rocking with his knees held to his chest.

"Pah. Sometimes you annoy me, little brother."

Turning to Kimi he said, "I won't be gone long. And don't think you can run, little bird. When I catch you, you'll wish you hadn't tried." His curling lip suggested he wanted her to try, and he left the door open.

Courage flowed through her veins making her feel dangerous. It felt like a wild animal lurked inside of her just waiting to get out. She imagined fangs and claws and supernatural strength that would tear his arms off his body. She would grow and tower over him. He's the one who would cringe and beg. She would be a beast—part tiger, part boar, part wolf.

Kimi shuddered. Springing from the platform, she grabbed the shard from where it lay on the floor at her feet. She might not be able to run far up the dark road without being caught, but she was getting good at hiding. Paju, lost in his misery, didn't notice her movement toward the door.

She hesitated, tempted to get her pack before taking several more steps to the door. Too late. Twigs snapped, and Kailì filled the doorway. One arm cradled a load of wood.

"Thought you could run, little bird?"

He dropped the wood, and his hand flashed out to imprison her left arm just above the elbow. Without thinking, she grabbed the pointed shard of her aunt's plate, reached across, and stabbed the back of his hand.

"Yama's demons," he exclaimed. "Not so fast, little badger," he said, menace pushing the words low and mean. He drew her to him and pulled back his bloody hand as though to hit her. Her right hand rose, holding the shard as a dagger. Tingling warmth flowed through her limbs, giving strength to her arms and back. She felt light and powerful. He seemed to grow smaller.

In the light of the dying fire, Kimi saw the shadow of her hand arch against the wall like the claw of a hideous beast. Her vision blurred as anger seared her mind. Anger for the harm done to her grandfather and aunt. Anger for Mister Cho's thievery. Anger at these men for destroying Xiao's crane. Kailì's eyes opened wide with horror, and she plunged the point of the claw into his left eye, then turned and ran out of the door. She left behind a bellow of pain and rage, and the sound of Paju whimpering.

She passed the clearing in two strides, leaves billowing in her wake. Turning onto the road north it seemed she floated above her body. The sounds from the hut seemed muffled, but her now sharp vision penetrated the thick darkness of the forest.

She took four more long strides before cries from the hut caught up to her ears. The noise came to her dimly—the door crashed back against the outside wall, carrying Kailì's swearing and Paju's wailing.

Run faster, she ordered her legs. Her gait seemed wrong. She felt suspended from the ground even though she could see the ruts and potholes. Odd, but she didn't have time to figure it out.

"Daughter of a whore, what have you done to me? What kind of devil are you?"

His words receded. She let instinct and fear carry her far up the road. Soon she heard only the huffing of her breath, and then not even that.

As the panic and rage began to ebb, her strength left her. She slowed as her vision faded. The forest appeared like stalking shadows. Her feet felt the hardness of the ground. She slowed to a walk, then stopped when she could no longer see the edges of the road.

She bent over, fists on her knees, as ragged breaths tore through her chest. Her right hand still held the shard, its sharp edges pressed into her palm. She slid the shard back into her pocket then peered at her hand—sticky with blood, but it was her hand. No claws. The vision had been a figment of her imagination born of fear and rage.

How long had she run? A few minutes? The ache in her legs and the shortness of her breath said it was much longer. Her arms and legs felt so heavy she couldn't stand much longer. She found a tree and slid down its trunk, crouching at its base. The cold crept into her clothing, prickling her skin.

She reached for her blanket, but almost all her belongings were in the cabin. She pulled her knees tighter to her chest in an effort to keep warm. Her prospects were dismal. Alone in the mountains with no blanket, no coat, no food, and no money.

To keep from shaking she rocked from side to side, feeling the bark of the tree brushing her back, holding her mother's medallion in her fist. At least Kailì hadn't seen the pendant.

After a while, her rocking slowed, her eyelids drooped, and she felt herself slipping into sleep.

Chapter Sixteen

Shi-lin was once more alone in the courtyard of the monastery when Kuan Yin came to her.

"I have grievous news," Kuan Yin said.

Shi-lin's heart faltered.

"I have found Tuan," she said. "He was attacked by thieves on his way to the city. Even now he sits before the God of Moats and Walls who will judge his life."

Shi-lin's heart was torn in two, one part she saved for the child she would bear, but the other part followed Tuan into death. She knew that once spring arrived and the hundred days of mourning were past, the God of Moats and Walls would send Tuan's soul to the heaven reserved for humans or would send him to Lord Yama, the God of Death and Rebirth. There he would wait the turn of the Celestial Wheel that would take him to his new life, and she would lose him forever. For though he had pledged love beyond death, Shi-lin had no illusions that she would find his spirit among the hundreds of thousands of souls reborn each year.

Shi-lin pinned the band of mourning to her sleeve. Her tears fell and heavy snow shrouded the mountain passes.

On the fortieth day since Tuan began his final trip, Shi-lin felt the tightening of her womb. Knowing that the labor would be difficult and that she might not survive, she made preparations for the child's future.

She called for Master Wu. Though he was the Tao Shih, the head of the monastery, he was also a healer of some renown. It was he who would attend her labor.

"Master Wu, there is a thing I must tell you. It is a thing only Tuan has known. I ask that you tell no others unless it is for the well-being of my child."

"What is this fearsome secret?" he asked.

"I am not as I seem. I came into this world as a dragon. I have taken the shape of a woman. If I return to dragon form to prove this, I will surely lose the babe. You must promise that if there comes a choice of one life over the other, you will choose the child's life. I have but half a heart now, and without the child, I would have none at all."

Master Wu agreed.

"If I die, you must promise me that she will be well educated and raised in kindness."

Master Wu stood and bowed to Shi-lin in great reverence.

She saw the vow in the old man's eyes and knew it was in his heart as well.

* * *

Kimi floated above her sleeping body. Icy dew clung to her as she slept.

Then she blinked and found herself once more sitting on the bench beside her carp pond in Kaisun. A gentle breeze carried golden leaves to her. A thread of peace wove its way through her. For a few minutes she could stop and forget everything that had happened.

Perhaps if she died, she could come to this place. It would be better than the Ten Hells. After all, the man had called her a devil. Part human, part beast. Evil.

"You are not evil, you know."

Startled, Kimi turned toward the sound.

It was the same woman she'd seen in other visions. Who was she anyway? Kimi always forgot to ask. She was sure the woman hadn't been there a minute ago. The visitor looked steadily back at Kimi with an expression that dared her to disagree.

"If I'm not evil, then what am I?"

"A dragon, of course."

Kimi laughed. Dragons and mysterious companions. *Fàng pì!* Kimi shook her head, but the woman didn't say anything more; she only arched an eyebrow. Somehow she didn't seem quite as old as Kimi had thought.

"Who are you? Are you my grandmother?"

"In a way I am everyone's mother and grandmother." The woman continued, "The bandit did not touch your spirit, Tengshe, only your body, and you did not harm him more than was necessary to free yourself. You could have, you know."

Kimi wanted to disagree, but hesitated. She remembered the feel of hitting the bandit—first on the hand, then in the eye. She'd been angry. She'd wanted to hurt him. The evil in her had wanted to rip his arms off, to see him cringe from her just like he'd made her cower from him.

The good girl Aunt Lu raised would have been patient and found another way to get free. Kimi shook her head. No, that isn't what would have happened.

"You are right," the woman said. "That patient girl would have been raped and held captive, sold, or killed. You are not evil. The darkness you believe to be in your soul is only your grief."

Grief wouldn't trigger a murderous rage.

"Grief manifests itself in many forms. Most people feel powerless. Those with real power seek to act. Your spirit is filled with that kind of power. You will see."

The woman had read her mind. She even knew her name. And was not old. The hair tucked neatly into her bun was glossy black. Not a strand of grey. How did she know so much about Kimi? Was this a dream? Kimi blinked and found herself hovering over her sleeping body. Another blink and she was back with the woman in the garden.

"The road ahead is going to be difficult. Do you want to turn back?"

Kimi did, but she had a promise to keep.

A ghost of a smile played on the lovely mouth of the stranger. "You may change your mind when you see how difficult the next day will be. There will be no shame if you choose to go back now." The lady's head tipped toward Kimi in a sign of respect.

So far she'd run away from the soldiers and a cabbage farmer and attacked a vagabond—nothing worthy of honor. She hadn't even taken good care of Hachi. Was her plan to go quickly in the mountains and return again just another form of escape? Did she really believe the monks would have the right medicine? Or that Xiao would willingly adopt an orphan?

"Xiao is looking for you," the woman continued. "He is worried. You should know that he has a great heart, and he loves you with all of it."

Kimi sighed. If only she knew the woman's words were true. As she remembered her conversation with Xiao in the garden, sour thoughts flooded Kimi's mind. "He has a funny way of showing it, arguing with me. Where were his words of love?"

The lady's laugh was gentle. "He might think you argued with him."

"He is so stern. There is stone where his heart is supposed to be."

"Are you sure?" The lady radiated a soothing aura. Her dress became a glorious gown—flowing lustrous white silk. She held a pitcher of water and a willow wand—the signs of the Goddess, Kuan Yin! Could it be possible she was a goddess? Kimi had never believed in gods, but what could she say if one stood before her? Not knowing what else to do, Kimi knelt.

Kuan Yin motioned with the willow wand for Kimi to rise. "You need to go back now. You've been too long away from your body. Be well, child. The road ahead is treacherous. If you wish to turn back, do it now. There will be no other chance. If the journey proves too difficult, remember the gods will honor the soul of one who tried so hard."

The Goddess faded along with the bench and the fishpond. Kimi slid back into her dream.

* * *

Groggy, with webs of sleep wrapping her mind, Kimi realized that she had been staring at the boulder in front of her for some time. In a gap between branches, she could see the underside of heavy clouds hanging over the forest. Frost edged the uppermost leaves that lay in a drift beside her. Her breath made puffs of cloud that floated away from her face. She rose slowly. Her achy body protested. Her arms dimpled with cold as she left the cradle of warmth she had built, and wispy tendrils of steam rose from the leaves where she had been huddled.

She extended her arm, half expecting to see scales covering it and to find curving claws where her fingers should be. But it was only a hand.

She, a dragon? Pah. It must have been the shadow of the shard she saw, not a claw. And talking to a goddess? Just a fever dream.

But then she noticed that blood streaked her fingers and stained the beds of her nails. Her stomach rebelled at the vivid memory—at the anger and hatred she'd felt, at the claw-like hand she'd seen in the shadow against the wall, at the look of terror on the man's face, the ease with which she'd penetrated his eye. She retched into the leaves at the base of the tree.

She wiped her mouth and stood on wavering legs. The vision or dream was rooted in her mind. Such a delightful fantasy, but fantasy nevertheless. Something had changed in her, something terrible, no matter how much her sleeping mind tried to find a nice way to explain it.

She walked back to the road and looked in both directions. The woman in her vision said this was her last chance to turn back. But she'd already made her decision to find Xiao and get medicine for Hachi. She frowned as a new thought blossomed in the back of her mind. She wanted Xiao even if she was mad at him. He had been like a brother through her childhood, but now she wanted him to love the way a man loves a woman. But maybe he wouldn't want her if he knew she'd almost killed a man.

She turned north, toward Xiao's home, and marched quickly up the frost-lined road, unencumbered by her heavy packs.

Not far off the road she found a frigid stream. The water made her fingers sting. She rubbed them hard with the edge of her jacket to get rid of the blood, which made them sting more.

While rubbing, the piece of her aunt's plate fell out of her pocket. She picked it up, avoiding the sharp point. It had no sign of blood. She shuddered at the memory of the shadowed claw. Her exhaustion must have made her see things that weren't there.

She returned the shard to her pocket and went back to scrubbing her hands, digging to get the nail beds clean. No matter how hard she tried, a rim of blood remained.

The day had been cold to start, but as she traveled it seemed to grow colder. The need to hurry added an urgent undertone to all her thoughts. Before long, she came abruptly out of the forest. A flat plateau spread out before her. The road was a beaten track between boulders with an expanse of wild grass on either side. Overhanging the meadow was a cloud so low it almost brushed the top of her head. Fine flakes of snow swirled, touching her face like the gentlest of whispers.

Turn back, they said.

No, she answered. Her future lay ahead.

The snow grew heavier and turned to fat flakes, laden with frosty water.

Her fingers turned red and the tip of her nose tingled and started to run. She took long strides, knowing she had a long way to go to get to the monastery. A day at least.

She didn't know if she could live through a night in the snow without a blanket or outer coat. Was this what the goddess meant? She walked faster.

The moonlike disk of the sun glowed through the low clouds. Soon even that disappeared behind the solid bank of grey clouds.

Before long her feet were sinking in the ankle-deep snow. Her toes and fingers grew numb. She pushed herself, finding tiny reserves of strength to keep moving. Her sides ached as she struggled to breathe the cold air.

The wind brought slivers of ice mixed with the snow. Sleet sliced her face. Moving was the only way to keep her clothes from freezing like a hard-cased icicle.

Walking became a lurching stumble. Her feet were so numb it felt as though she walked on the bones of her legs. She put one foot in front of the other, sometimes staggering to keep her balance on the slick path. If she stopped, she would never live through the night. Even with her uncertain future, Kimi didn't want to die.

No sunset. No warning as night fell. The sky darkened to heavy gray and then to charcoal. How long had she been walking? Hours probably, or maybe minutes. She knew she wouldn't survive another night, so she began to run in the cart tracks, lifting her knees high to clear the newly fallen snow. Surely she must be getting close. She had to be.

She reached the first of the pines as the light faded to a soft black.

Darkness reduced the world to a luminescent thread of white road. She'd forgotten where she was going and why. All that mattered were the tracks in front of her. She didn't realize they'd turned until she almost ran into the front of a barn that blocked her way. A footpath led away and up a steep slope of stairs. She saw a thin line of light on the side of the barn. A door. She pushed until the door gave way, sending a spill of light onto the snow at her feet. She stumbled across the threshold and fell into the room. It felt like falling into a warm bath.

She called out hoarsely, her voice not much stronger than a kitten's. An oil lantern hung from a beam in the center of the small barn. But she couldn't see anyone. Disappointment made her limbs even weaker. Her fingers throbbed as blood returned to them.

"Hsing, close the door, will you?" A man's voice called out from behind the stalls where two shaggy ponies lay in a heaping pile of straw. The room smelled of manure and grain and warm animal.

"Who are you?" asked the man when he spotted Kimi.

"Where is Xiao? I need him." Reaching the end of her strength, she collapsed onto the floor.

Chapter Seventeen

For two days, Shi-lin struggled to deliver the child. Kuan Yin came to Master Wu, bringing elixirs and herbs. Still, the child would not loosen its hold on Shi-lin's womb.

Kuan Yin held her as Shi-lin fought her body's urge to revert to dragon form in order to flee the pain. Shi-lin kept the womanly form with an iron will.

On the dawn of the third morning, as the sun sent its first rays through Shi-lin's window, the child was born at last.

The tiny girl was perfect. Shi-lin touched the softness of the little cheek and smelled the sweetness of the child's breath. A dragon tear fell on the baby's head as Shi-lin's eyes closed, and her life slipped away.

Shi-lin's soul flew to the heaven reserved for dragons.

* * *

The heaven was as beautiful as she had imagined it in her youth. There were large pavilions, open gardens, and music perfumed the air with rippling sounds like the splash of water from a thousand fountains. She appreciated none of the beauty of the dragon heaven. In the course of four unlucky weeks she had lost her husband and been separated from her daughter.

Her first thought was for her child. Tuan was dead, she was dead, at least the child might live. She called upon the goddess, Kuan Yin, but the goddess did not come.

* * *

Unwelcome light slid under the lids of Kimi's eyes. The light came, along with cold air, from a square brick of carved stone that served as window and vent.

Lying on her side, her eyes traced the arcs and lines the mason had made in the block. Cold radiated through the spaces in the stone's design as easily as the light, and Kimi felt the chill air stroking her face with invisible hands. The crisp touch on her cheeks soothed her. Blankets sealed her body in a cocoon of warmth. Too hot, actually. She folded back some of the covers.

She heard a gentle cough—somebody cleared his throat. She turned to the sound, holding herself up on shaky arms. A little monkey of a man with a book in his lap was sitting in a chair beside her bed. A holy man. The thought took a moment to settle in her mind. She had made it to the monastery. Weak with relief, she lay on her side, studying the man.

"Good morning," he said. His voice was rich and deep, surprising for such a small, old man. She almost laughed.

"I'm Kimi. Thank…" Her words were interrupted by a deep, painful cough that seemed to rise from her toes like a spasm.

He smiled. "I am Master Wu. Welcome to Morning Song."

"Are you the same Master Wu that Xiao spoke about when we were children?"

"Yes, I am that Master Wu."

"Did he live in the monastery? All he ever said was that he lived with Master Wu not far from Pianshan."

"I am not surprised. Xiao is a very private person, but you already know that."

A sense of urgency filled Kimi. "How long have I been here?" Her voice was scratchy. Her throat burned.

"Two days."

She sat up. "Oh, no! It might be too late. Do you have medicine for a terrible fever and cough? I left a sick child, Hachi, in the care of a farmer. I must get back to him."

"Yes, we have medicine, but you are too ill to go anywhere right now. Besides, the roads are impassable, at least for a few days. You must be patient. The gods will care for the boy."

Kimi clenched her jaw. "Hachi might die if I don't get medicine to him soon."

"Try not to worry. The young are strong." Master Wu reached to the table again and poured a small cup of water to which he added a pinch of brownish powder from the crucible.

She eyed him suspiciously. "This isn't going to make me sleep again, is it?"

"No, it is just something to chase away the infection in your chest."

She took the cup he offered. The water felt wonderful on her sore throat. Other than a slightly smoky flavor, it tasted like plain water. She lowered herself back to the bed. He adjusted the covers so that they were back in place, accompanying his action with a look of admonishment so similar to Aunt Lu's it made her blink. He meant for her to stay under the blankets, even if she drowned in perspiration.

Her long, white gown was damp around the neck and under her arms as if a small river ran down her back. But the mound of blankets wasn't precisely the cause. Her eyes burned, and the breath leaving her nostrils felt hot on her lips. Bandages wrapped her feet and ankles. Her feet felt like sausages left too long in the sun—swollen and probably red from the way they stung. They had not fared well. At least they weren't numb anymore.

Kimi used all her strength to speak again. "Master Wu, I came all this way to find Xiao. Does he live far? I must see him."

"Be calm, child. We sent for Xiao."

Kimi sighed. "That's wonderful, but how did you know to send for him?"

Master Wu gently pushed her shoulder to the bed, shaking his head but still smiling. "You asked for him when you first arrived, and you've called his name many times in your sleep. I know that you are Kimi. I know my good friend, Chen Tung—the man you call Grandfather—and his sister are dead. I know you are worried about Hachi. I know you are very angry with Mister Cho. I know that this piece of porcelain is very important to you." He motioned to the table where the shard of Aunt Lu's plate rested. "That is a story I want to hear. And I know that you are a very sick young woman who needs to rest."

What else had she said about Xiao? Master Wu still grinned at her, so it must not have been anything too hateful.

"Where is Xiao? The Japanese…"

"Ah. Xiao would not let himself get caught by the Japanese, if that is your concern. He went to Pianshan to look for you. He will be back in another day."

"How did he know to look there?" Kimi's head began to throb, making it hard to talk.

Master Wu patted her again. "Xiao will explain when he returns. In the meantime you need to rest." He moved to the table and poured a small amount of brownish liquid from the elixir bottle into a small teacup, added some water, and made her drink it. It tasted awful.

The kindly monk patted the thin book he'd placed on the table, but didn't take it. He left, closing the door behind him.

* * *

When Kimi woke again, she felt much stronger. A young monk sat sewing in the chair next to her bed. He was making neat stitches in a grey smock that lay across his lap. Another smock lay in a basket at his feet. When he looked up and noticed her, he took a stitch to anchor his needle, then rose, setting the unfinished work into the basket. "Are you thirsty?" he asked.

She nodded. The second medicine he'd given her must have included something to make her sleep.

She eyed the cup the monk held out to her. "Is that plain water or does it contain medicine?"

"It is just water."

Kimi drank the offered water, then asked for more. Her throat didn't feel as raw as before. She felt as if she'd slept for a lifetime. *Fàng pì!* Would she never get back to Hachi?

"I will get Master Wu. He asked to be called when you woke." The young monk picked up his sewing and hurried out the door.

Master Wu entered the room in a rush, bringing an aura of energy and wellbeing with him.

He felt her forehead for fever. "Gone." He took the seat beside her and looked at her expectantly.

"Has Xiao returned?"

"Yes, he returned hours ago. But I told him you would sleep for a long time, so he left to prepare his house for your wedding. I also told him about the sick boy, but I made him understand that your health is too fragile to spend three days exposed to the cold and snow."

Kimi's sense of urgency swelled. She reached toward the master. "My health doesn't matter. When can I see Xiao?"

"He should be back within an hour."

Master Wu was pushing the edges of her patience. She thought about getting dressed and chasing after Xiao. But when she flexed her toes she realized her feet weren't ready for another walk in the snow. Kimi hated being dependent on other people. She lay back against her pillows, resigned to waiting it out.

Master Wu folded his hands neatly in his lap. How knotted his hands were—small hands with ridges of bone at each joint. His animated face made him seem younger. Speaking with him, it was easy to forget his age. "Tell me of your journey," he said. "From the words that came as you dreamed, it seems to me that you had great adventures."

There was a hard edge to her laugh. "Great adventures? That's not what I'd call them. It's been more like a journey through Hell."

She told him of her travels, leaving nothing out except her anger at Xiao and the visions—folly anyway. Talking to a goddess? Not likely. Before long she'd told him about piercing the bandit's eye, though her voice shook while she relived the memory. His mouth stayed neutral, neither frowning nor pinched in mocking humor. He didn't interrupt her story with questions, though she saw the eagerness in his eyes to know more.

"It was horrible. How could I have done such a thing? Afterwards, I remembered the shadow of a clawed hand on the wall. It must have just been the piece of plate tricking my eyes, but it looked like a claw." After so much talking, Kimi coughed, deep and hard. Her ribs ached.

Master Wu waited for her coughing to end. "This bothers you? Hurting the bandit?"

"Yes. It bothers me. Only an evil person would want to take a man's eye." The wretched feeling came back over her. She'd never felt such hatred for another human being.

He shook his head. "You do not understand, child. You are not an evil person. It is both natural and honorable to protect yourself." He tipped his head toward his shoulder. The mirth left his eyes. "The spirit that fills you is not evil. It is not a hungry ghost, angry that its life was taken. You are not evil, if that is what you think."

The hollow, churning feeling in her stomach returned. "If it wasn't evil, then why is my soul so black that I wanted to hurt someone, maybe even kill him?" Then, remembering Gota, she added, "In fact, I have killed a man. How is that not evil?"

He closed his eyes for a moment.

"You do not know, do you?"

"Know what?"

"That medallion you wear. What do you think it means?"

Kimi pulled the medallion from her gown and frowned, confused by the sudden change in the conversation. "My mother left it with me when I was a baby. I assume it was hers, but Aunt Lu never knew or never said."

"It was your mother's, but the pearl it carries is you. You are a dragon's child. Your mother was a dragon, but the rest of the story needs to wait until we have more time to discuss her. For now you should be grateful. Your mother's blood will help you heal."

Dragons. Is that all anyone thought about? "I'm not a dragon. I was born in the year of the rat."

Another fit of coughing shook her.

"You possess the spirit of a dragon. You can perform magic."

She gritted her teeth. "I cannot...perform...magic."

A grin turned up one corner of his wide mouth. "Perhaps not in ways you recognize yet."

Master Wu was deluded, just like the woman in the dreams—the woman who existed only in her imagination. Kimi's mind had reached for a magic way out of her troubles, so she'd invented a goddess. Except this time she wasn't half asleep. Master Wu had added a dragon ancestor. Ridiculous!

Kimi lowered her head and adjusted the blankets in her lap, angrily picking at the small patterns of the stitching. The master was old. So old that his reasoning was muddled. Xiao would come soon. Then she wouldn't need to trouble Master Wu anymore.

He motioned her to continue with her story. Kimi squared her shoulders and finished. Not much else to tell—just the terrible snow and ice. When he asked, she didn't remember finding the monastery.

"You scared the young man tending to the ponies. You were burning with fever. Now you are here, and all is well. Xiao will be here soon, and in a few days, after you are stronger, he can take you to find your friend Hachi."

He rose and bent over the table, readying more medicine. "No, it does not contain poppy."

Kimi swallowed the medicine in a rush. It tasted bitter. She closed her eyes and slumped sideways onto the pillow, hoping Xiao would come soon and take her to Hachi.

Chapter Eighteen

She went to the gate of the heaven, hoping she could leave and determine her daughter's well-being. To her dismay, the way was barred. She entreated the guards, and when that failed, attempted to bribe them. They would not give her passage.

She implored the goddess to hear her, but the goddess was not there to listen. Shi-lin feared the goddess had forsaken her and she'd never learn her daughter's fate.

If she lived would Master Wu follow her instructions? Would she be raised among the homeless? If her daughter possessed magic would anyone teach her the way of it? Shi-lin grieved for this loss more than all others. She would not be able to guide her child as she grew into a woman. Shi-lin would never hold her grandchild.

Shi-lin spoke to a heavenly messenger who was waiting at the gate. She sent him to seek the goddess. When he again appeared two days later he informed Shi-lin that the goddess was not in the heavenly realms.

Shi-lin burned incense to speed her prayers to the goddess' ears, but Kuan Yin still did not respond.

* * *

After she'd slept a long while, Kimi felt better. She dressed herself, finding clothing in the carved chest in the room. Women's clothing. Beautiful clothing. Beneath layers of jackets she wore a long, dark-blue skirt and a heavy silk top of light blue with white cranes embroidered along the edges.

Her feet were still tender and pink, but they were mostly healed. What had Master Wu said? Her dragon blood would help her heal faster. Kimi cringed. First the goddess had told her the preposterous story, and now Master Wu. Could it be true? The claw. The scales. The feeling of strength. The sensation of flying. No. There had to be some other explanation. She did her best to put it out of her mind.

Kimi went to the temple to see if Xiao had returned. She sat just inside the temple door where she could see the stairs leading down to the road below. In front of her she could see the refectory, the teahouse, and the little knoll of garden where Master Wu often sat.

Her anger and frustration mounted. Where was Xiao?

She looked up as squawking magpies flew past the door to the temple. She filled her time reading the book of poetry Master Wu left in her room. But the sound of the raucous birds distracted her, and she lowered the book to her lap.

The poetry was about a mother's hope. At first, the poems had been full of joy. But then, toward the end of the book, they had been tinged with sadness. These suited Kimi's mood better, and she read them slowly, letting each word fill her mind.

> The last chrysanthemum hangs from a bent stem
> Golden brown leaves drift against the garden wall
> A single crane flies south to its summer home
> So my saddened heart longs for you
> A single crane. Like Kimi.

Excited voices diverted Kimi's attention. Two arriving monks stood at the top of the steps surrounded by a half dozen other monks badgering the new arrivals.

A tall, slender young traveler answered excitedly: "We were warned, but we didn't believe it. All of Pianshan is held. Barricades block all the roads."

Kimi's breath caught. Was Hachi safe? Another thought struck her. What about Xiao? Perhaps he'd been harmed, or worse. That would explain why he hadn't come yet.

A figure frosted with snow came toward her from the opposite side of the courtyard. Master Wu. When he sat down beside her, a deep voice emerged from the wool muffler. Holding a gloved hand under his arm, he pulled until a brown hand emerged. With it, he unwrapped the muffler exposing most of this face. The corners of her mouth twitched as she held back laughter.

"Ah, go ahead and laugh," he said. "But you are young. Let us see how you will do in the cold when you are old."

His face grew serious as he touched the cover of the book of poetry, then looked at her. Kimi thought he would say something about it, but he let the moment pass.

"What worries you?" he asked.

"I want Xiao to get here so we can take the medicine to Hachi. I'm worried something may have happened to him."

"Xiao is back. I am sure he will be up as soon as he unloads the cart at his house."

Kimi felt some relief, but then her anger returned. Xiao seemed to be in no hurry to see her.

"Xiao's farm, is it far from here?" When Xiao had described it to her, she hadn't had a clear picture of the distances.

"A day," he said.

"If it's a day from here, how will he be here soon?"

Master Wu busied himself with unwrapping his scarf, giggling as if something was funny. "Do you know about Xiao's latest folly?"

"You mean planting potatoes?"

He laughed. "This summer, he cleared some land so he could plant potatoes. He loves potatoes. He knows nothing of farming, and the season is so short that I am not sure they will thrive, but he assures me that he will be successful." He shook his head, clearly not sharing Xiao's confidence, though just as clearly amused by it.

Master Wu leaned toward her, as though to share a secret. His eyes danced. Kimi leaned in as well, grabbing the book as it started to slip off her lap. "He read about growing potatoes in a book. Such silliness. One does not learn to grow things from a book any more than one learns to fish that way. Do you think the potatoes or the fish follow the rules a writer puts on his pages? It is a thing the Westerners do—write books on every trivial topic. Have they no fathers or uncles to teach them these things?"

His words reminded her of Grandfather.

"You will like Xiao's home," he continued. "It has good *Feng Shui*, a home of great happiness once. You can see the sun rise over the lake." His arms swayed over his head as he traced the motion of the sun. "The deer used to come to the lake every evening. I wonder if he has restored the garden. You could watch the deer from there. And sometimes a tiger would come to the lake."

She took in a quick breath.

"Never worry. The home and the land around it are protected."

"What's protecting them?"

"Dragon magic."

"Even if there were dragons, how could they protect all the land around a home?"

Master Wu put on his gloves. "Someday you will believe. So what do you think, Kimi? Will you marry a potato farmer?"

She thought about Biyu's quiet dignity, but her heart hammered "no, no, no." She picked up the book from her lap and hugged it to her. "I'm sure Xiao will be successful if he wishes to be. Perhaps he will find farming doesn't suit him."

"Aha! We agree," he said with such emphasis she almost jumped. "Even if his potatoes grow, he will see they are not his destiny."

With his finger waggling, Mr. Wu said, "And while you may work in the dirt and learn to weave, these things are not your destiny, either. You were made for grander things."

"If the last two weeks are an example, my destiny appears to be doomed."

Master Wu turned his head, staring out the Temple door. "Ah. Here he is now."

Coming from the stairs, Xiao crossed the courtyard, gliding over the snow with the same formal posture that had annoyed her in Kaisun. Kimi felt her face grow warm and hoped Master Wu hadn't seen her blushing.

Xiao tipped his head to Kimi, then stopped in front of Master Wu and paid his respects with a low bow. Proper, Kimi thought with annoyance. She gritted her teeth. Nothing more than a nod to his bride who had spent long miserable days on the road.

Master Wu gave Xiao a stern look. "I expected you this morning."

Xiao spread his hands. "The cart had to be pried free twice."

"I was about to send Kimi back to bed. Fresh air is good, so long as it is brief. You may talk to her for a short while, but then you are to bring her back to her room."

Good. She hoped she could convince Xiao to leave soon to get Hachi. Maybe they could go right after lunch.

Master Wu wound the scarf back over his mouth and pushed the hat down firmly on his head so that the furry rim came down just above his eyes.

A rush of cold air filled the spot where he'd been sitting, and it didn't seem to leave when Xiao sat beside her. Xiao removed his gloves, tucking them into his coat pockets, then he folded his long, slim fingers in his lap and became still. When he spoke, the deepness of his voice startled her like it had in Kaisun. It wasn't as deep as Master Wu's, but it had a fuller sound — echoing like the ringing of a heavy bell. "I am pleased you arrived safely."

"Safely? I'm still alive if that's what you mean." She closed her eyes and swallowed her irritation. He was trying to be polite, but it felt to her as if he were speaking to someone he didn't know.

"I am grieved to learn of your grandfather's death. I respected Master Chen," he said, a twitch of anguish in his voice.

Bitterness filled her mouth. Maybe he couldn't have known. But her feelings said he should have. Yet that wasn't her most serious problem at the present time. "Xiao, it's urgent that I go back to a farm just north of Pianshan. Hachi, a little boy I helped, is very ill, and he won't be safe if the Japanese come. I need medicine and a cart to go there and come back with the boy."

"Master Wu says you are unwell."

Kimi drew her hands into fists. "Master Wu doesn't understand how serious Hachi's condition is."

"We will go tomorrow. It will be best if we get an early start."

Frustration peaked to anger. How she hated being dependent on others. "Tomorrow could be too late."

"We'll go tomorrow," he repeated. "Now you need to return to your bed and rest. I will see you tonight at the Festival of Universal Salvation."

Kimi stamped her foot, not caring about a festival. *Fàng pì!*

* * *

She had a change of heart after a long nap. The festival had always been important to her, and now more than ever. She and Xiao and the monks went to a pond not far from the path into the forest.

Kimi brought the two paper boats she'd made. Xiao brought little paper boats as well. Kimi remembered festivals in Kaisun where the lake glowed with hundreds of boats. Tonight the lake should have been covered with thousands of boats, one for each of Kaisun's souls so that they would be freed to rise to heaven. But almost no one lived to perform the ritual.

When it was Kimi's turn, she took one of the paper boats – the one for Grandfather - and lit a candle, anchoring it with a few drops of wax so it wouldn't fall. She pushed it out on the pond to join the others. She repeated the ritual for the other boat—the one for Aunt Lu's soul.

Her two boats joined the many others. Like fairies dancing on the water, the boats nearly filled the pond. Kimi's heart spilled over as she grieved for Grandfather and Aunt Lu. After launching his own boats, Xiao came and put his arm around Kimi. She buried her face in his chest until the moon rose and she shivered from the cold.

After the ceremony Kimi sat propped up in bed to read before going to sleep. Soft pearl moonlight filtered through the window screen and made shadows of her hands across the beautiful calligraphy. She had turned to the back again and read the poems most filled with longing for a lost lover. Kimi had never known the kind of love the poems expressed, but felt she could understand the ones that spoke of a broken soul.

She had to get past the rigid gatekeeper of Xiao's emotions, but she didn't know how. If their relationship wasn't soulful love as the book described, she hoped theirs would be something akin to friendship. She hoped he would understand her need to educate orphan girls. And keep Hachi.

Chapter Nineteen

On the day the child would have been one month old and receiving her first gifts, Kuan Yin finally came to Shi-lin.

Shi-lin clutched the hem of the goddess' gown. "Dear goddess, can you tell me of my daughter?"

"Rest easy in your heart. Your daughter is well. I have taken on the burden of her care myself. It is that which has kept me from coming to you."

"But if you are here . . ."

"Do not fret. Master Wu has become proficient in her care."

"What will become of her now?"

"At Master Wu's recommendation, when she is old enough, I will present myself to an old scholar and his sister. They will love her as their own granddaughter and will see that she grows to have a strong mind and a kind heart."

For a moment Shi-Lin's heart was full, but then she thought of Tuan. He would never see his child.

Once Shi-lin was at peace regarding her daughter, she turned her attention to the fate of her husband.

She spoke to the goddess, Kuan Yin. "Dear goddess, you have restored half of my heart, but I grieve for the other half. Is there no way that Tuan can join me here? Certainly he is worthy of the right to remain with his wife and to be united with his child when she passes into heaven."

Promising nothing, Kuan Yin left the dragon heaven to seek Tuan's spirit in the afterlife.

* * *

Xiao came to Kimi's room early the following morning, just after she'd finished her breakfast. His posture was stiffer than usual, if that were possible. He had the look of someone with an unpleasant task to perform. So much for an enthusiastic greeting.

She swallowed her annoyance. "Are we taking the medicine to Hachi?"

"Yes. But may we talk first? Just for a moment."

"I've waited long enough. We need to go now." She rose and stamped her foot.

Xiao's expression remained calm. "Master Wu is gathering winter clothes and the medicine for the boy. Put on your coat and boots. We can go to the teahouse where we can talk."

Kimi jammed her arms into her overcoat.

Xiao escorted her into the courtyard. Once more the sky turned grey, the clouds pregnant with snow. Trumpeting cranes flew overhead drawing her eyes sharply upward. Three cranes flew low. At the head of the formation the body of a lone black crane blended so well with the dense grey sky that for an instant all she saw were the wings and tail feathers, black as night. Her heart skipped a beat as she remembered the head of the fragile jade crane snapping off in the hands of the bandit's younger brother. For the briefest moment, she feared the bird had escaped and flown into the winter sky without its body.

"Ancestors, help us," she whispered. The words were out of her mouth before she thought. *Fàng pì!* She wasn't one of those silly women in front of the laundry in Kaisun. She was not superstitious.

Xiao's touch on her elbow startled her. His brow creased in worry lines as he examined her face. "What is it, Kimi?"

In a hushed voice she said, "The women in Kaisun said they saw a black crane before the Japanese soldiers came."

"Your aunt told me of this; she seemed very concerned." Xiao urged Kimi forward, squeezing her elbow a bit too hard.

The door to the teahouse was like so many other doors with a carved tiger on one side and a carved dragon on the other to protect the house from evil spirits.

Just inside the door were pegs to hold their coats. Each peg had a carved dragon head. Kimi shrugged her coat off and felt a zing of satisfaction when it covered one of the heads.

She studied the room. Pillars, painted with images from China's past, held up the roof. Strong beams braced them, each beam carved with a mythological creature in vibrant indigo, vermillion, and gold paints. The ceiling showed paintings of clouds, dragons, and vivid rainbows of sunrise and sunset and a bright sprinkling of stars between.

Dragons again. Everywhere dragons.

Perhaps, as Aunt Lu thought, they had once been real. That didn't mean they had magical powers. People liked tales of magic and may have embellished them until dragons could do the most unlikely things—swallow the moon, bring storms, cause drought, walk on the clouds, appear as men, and become invisible.

Appear as men. Become invisible. The Japanese hadn't found her in the shed. She squirmed. There had to be another explanation.

Charcoal braziers in the corners kept the room warm. A tea service had been placed at the center of a square table directly in the middle of the room. The service included a plate of rice cakes, mounded, keeping the secret of its sweet bean paste, a kind she liked. They must have been brought from Pianshan because she couldn't imagine them coming from the monk's kitchen. The monks ate well, but plainly.

Kimi scooted her chair forward and rushed through the serving of tea. It seemed ironic to be doing something so mundane when her future would likely be the topic of discussion. What did Xiao want to talk about?

She stared straight ahead and touched the side of the teacup for something to do with her hands. The cup, as fragile as rice paper, burned her fingertips.

She looked up to see if Xiao was impatient, but avoided looking directly into his eyes. Had Master Wu told Xiao the preposterous tale about her being a dragon? If so, he would never want to marry her.

He slid his teacup forward, but instead of taking a sip to be polite, he turned the cup a quarter turn and let his hands fall in his lap.

"I regret I left Kaisun when I did. If I had known the Japanese would come to Kaisun…I will never be at peace over the death of Master Chen and Aunt Lu, or over your difficult journey. I should have stayed."

Kimi hadn't expected that his first words would be an apology. Finally. Something personal.

His composure broke. Tears formed in his eyes and he blinked them away.

Kimi's feelings of abandonment wavered. She had the overwhelming urge to comfort him and she spoke before her mind could tell her to be cautious. "It wouldn't have mattered. Grandfather was too ill to go, and Aunt Lu wouldn't go without him. They would have died anyway."

The words startled her. She cringed. She should be telling this to herself. She wasn't guilty, either. But her heart didn't feel that way.

Xiao shook his head, his face becoming more pained. "He did not need to die in that manner. He should have died in peace, not have his life ripped away from him by an enemy. I was a fool. I paid no attention to the movement from the south."

His fists clenched, revealing the depth of his sorrow. Kimi took a sip of tea. Before, she had wanted to see emotion on his face. Now it was hard to watch.

He continued. "What troubles me most is that I would make the same decision if the opportunity were presented again. I had to do my duty."

"What duties? You told me you left the court. What duty was so important?"

Xiao looked back at her with sharp glints flashing in his golden eyes. "The greater threat from the Japanese was from Dandong, where they ferried their troops from Korea. From there they could strike into the heart of Manchuria. I had to warn the magistrates in Mukden, or the Imperial Summer Palace would have been destroyed."

This time it looked like he was pleading for understanding.

"I came back and tried to locate you. I searched the road to Pianshan and the city itself, but there were too many refugees. I did not think you would come this far with winter approaching."

Kimi pressed her palms firmly on the table, ready to rise, but finding she lacked the strength. Slumping back in her chair, her hands fell loosely onto her lap. What was he saying? His story didn't make sense. Three cities in three days? And how had he avoided the Japanese? He couldn't have visited all those places in such a short time, yet that's what his story seemed to imply.

He shifted in his seat, looking down. "Matters have not been well between you and me."

"Why are you so enamored with potatoes? Why must we live in these mountains?"

His body stayed frozen. "I can do more good living here, where my movements are free. Matters in the world are not favorable, and I believe they will be even less so in the future. I require the freedom to help in the best way I can, and that means I must live away from cities."

"How can you help anybody hiding in hills like this? You can't even share your education by taking students. Were all those years of training a waste?"

He leaned forward like a tiger about to pounce, and Kimi leaned back. "My education is not a waste," he said with passion. "I do not hide in these mountains. I met with officials in Mukden one day, went to Peking the second day, and searched for you on the road to Pianshan on the third." Drops of saliva flew from his mouth. "I do not waste my time on trivial matters."

"You're speaking figuratively. You didn't really travel to three cities."

"I did exactly that. I move from place to place with little more than a thought."

"Just how do you do that?"

He leaned even farther across the table, his voice dropping to a cold, even delivery that pounded each word like a hammer on stone. "By magic. And you can do the same.

Dragons, Kimi. We are dragons. Master Wu knew your mother, but he didn't tell me until a few years ago, long after I'd left your home."

All the light in the room was sucked into an open pit in Kimi's middle. She stood and spread her arms wide. "I'm not a dragon, but I am evil. I killed one man and put out the eye of another. A hungry ghost has control of my soul—perhaps the spirit of a person killed brutally in Kaisun. The spirit must have suffered like Mei did. But there is no magic. It isn't possible to go from place to place with nothing more than a thought."

Xiao sprang to his feet. "No, you are not evil! Nothing has possessed your soul. Your soul is, and always has been, half-dragon." His arm swept out, pointing to the walls. He continued in a softer tone. "Look about you. This place has been a friend to dragons for many hundreds of years."

Anger pushed back the empty feeling, but she knew her voice sounded desperate. "The myths aren't real. They are just stories. Tales for children." She needed him to be rational—to deny this fantasy. She needed his strength, his understanding. She needed his love, so why did she have such a hard time accepting it?

He reached out and took her hand. She tried to pull away, but he held on firmly.

With his left hand he pointed at her shirt. "Whose clothes do you wear? Master Wu told me of the book he gave you. Who wrote that book, Kimi? Who wrote so hopefully of a child and then of such despair at the loss of her husband? It was your mother. Whose house have I made ready for you? A house that remained empty for all the years since your parents died. Master Wu knows you were dragon born, but he told no one. The medallion you wear was your mother's—a gift from your father."

Kimi gasped, her fingers brushing the medallion. "How do you know all this?"

"Master Wu told me and I believe him," he said, his golden eyes penetrating her heart. "We are alike, you and I."

Kimi's breath quickened. She didn't want him to go on. She didn't want to hear what he had to say next.

"I am a dragon, like you," Xiao whispered.

Kimi turned away. "You're wrong." She looked at Xiao, her eyes angry, begging him to stop. This wasn't right. If he did love her, he wouldn't frighten her with false tales. She tried to pull her hand away, but he held it fast.

His voice became quiet. His golden eyes glowed. She wanted him to take his words back, to make the world orderly once more. She had come so far and suffered so much. For what? A man who couldn't tell the difference between truth and fantasy?

"You must believe. Dragon blood travels in your veins. It travels in mine. We were meant to be together."

If only this were true. "I always hoped we could be together someday. But don't you see now that it's impossible? You believe in magic. And I don't."

"I shall prove magic to you. Watch…"

He held his left hand before her face. Green sparks flew. The outline of his hand changed, the edges blurring.

Heat swelled in Kimi's body. The image before her began to coalesce into the translucent shape of a claw. The bandits. The claw. Terror gripped her.

Green scales spread. They encased his arm and crept to the convergence where the arm joined with his claws. Dreadful obsidian talons curved to sharp points as the form became solid.

Ancestors, protect me, her mind shouted silently, her heart pounding. Kimi pushed herself to her feet and stumbled backward over her chair. She ran out the door and down the covered walkway.

Monks followed her as she ran across the courtyard. When she heard Xiao's voice calling her, she ran faster. He had the same claws and scaly skin she'd seen on her own arm when she had attacked Gota and the forest ruffians.

Chapter Twenty

Kuan Yin went to the God of Moats and Walls for the district of Pianshan.

She presented herself at the door to his office, but as he was merely a demi-god, Kuan Yin dispensed with the formalities quickly.

"I come to discuss the fate of one of your citizens. It has been two turnings of the moon since Tuan, the woodcarver, died. I wish to intercede in his next appointment."

"I have no memory of such a person. The influenza has struck Pianshan, and many souls have come to me for judgment. I cannot remember them all."

He bade his clerk to bring him the ledger. When he found the entry, he shook his head.

"I see that his case has already been judged: he has been sent to Lord Yama, God of Death and Rebirth, to await his turn on the Celestial Wheel. There is no more that I can do. You must discuss this with Lord Yama." He closed the ledger with a thump.

"You judge hastily these days," the goddess said, barely containing her fury. "What of the hundred days of grieving?"

The god shrugged. "No one prayed for intercession. I may use my discretion in such cases."

"May your elevation be so hastily judged and with so little compassion."

* * *

Kimi's breath came in gasps as she ran through the ankle-deep snow. She hurried down the forest path without regard for where she went. Branches whipped her. Her hair streamed out behind her. Cold air squeezed her laboring chest. Finally, exhaustion slowed her steps.

Before her eyes registered the movement, a tiger filled the path ahead, hovering over the carcass of a gutted deer. Shock blurred all clear thought.

The tiger's gold eyes issued a dangerous warning—do not proceed. Kimi stopped so fast she nearly toppled over. She took one step forward to brace herself. The tiger growled deep in his throat, guarding the fresh kill, his bloody red mouth circling bared teeth.

She stepped back.

The tiger's flank rippled as he leaned back, prepared to leap.

Kimi's heart faltered and her knees weakened. The tingles in her hands spread up her arms and down her legs. Then the transformation began. A flash of terror filled her. No. It couldn't be true.

The tiger growled.

Her vision sharpened. Now every detail was visible—every hair on the tiger's whiskered mouth, the black lines that circled its eyes and pooled beside his nose like coal-black tears, the white fur that stretched from his chin and spilled down his chest, and the tufts of amber hair between his toes.

Beauty and power. Her body trembled, sensing his terrible defiance.

Strength flooded her arms and legs. Blue-scaled arms reached down to the leafy track far below, arms that ended in three sharp talons. Kimi felt her mouth widen, and she tried to imagine how she must look with a fearsome grimace on her face. Her head stretched forward, extending beyond her arms in the front, with her body trailing behind. Concentrating, she could feel a tail at the farthest end of her body. She made it twitch. A terrible roar grew in her throat as she crouched low and centered her weight, hunching to strike.

The tiger's ears lay back, and a huge paw thrust forward in a warning swipe. She answered his advance with a swipe of her own, pushing his paw aside.

The tiger sprang, and she leaped to intercept him, turning so that when they collided her shoulder pushed him aside, narrowly missing his outstretched claws. His powerful body landed in the bushes, snapping winter-brittle twigs. He pulled himself forward and brought his legs tight under his belly. His tail swished from side to side. Lips tightened across his jaw, showing teeth that gleamed.

Kimi cowered inside. His next attack would be brutal. A surge of power rippled through her body, giving her mind strength. She had nothing to fear.

She loomed over him, many times his size. A deep rumbling thrummed through her chest. The tiger pulled back onto his hind legs, issuing his own growl, and flew at her. As she turned to push him aside again, his claws raked her shoulder.

Kimi growled again. This time anger and pain embellished the sound, and the growl became a fearsome roar, even to her ears. She'd had enough. With one spiked hand she sent him rolling down the path. When he came to his feet, he shook his head and ran away into the forest.

Victory! She shook her immense head and felt muscles loosen all the way down her body.

In the trampled snow, a deer lay on its side with its head arched back. The black eyes stared toward her, unblinking. Its throat was savaged. Red blood splashed on the bushes and onto the fresh snow. More blood oozed from the gash in the deer's belly where its entrails lay exposed. A sickening odor overpowered Kimi.

She leaped over the deer and flew down the path. Urgency pounded her brain like the beating of a heart. She had lived with fear for so many days; it had become the cardinal point in her life. No place was safe. No person was safe. She ran from fear itself, terror driving her deeper and deeper into the forest.

Awareness of the world came back slowly. She wasn't cold, despite the drifts of snow closing off most of the path. The pain in her shoulder broke its way into her mind. It throbbed in time with her running. Growing stronger, it overrode the fear. Kimi pushed the pain aside and concentrated on each step.

She careened down the unfamiliar path in a blur. Her feet didn't touch the ground. Only they weren't feet but four massive legs with curving claws instead of toes. And she loomed above them. In addition to seeing straight ahead, she could also see to the side and partway down her long, arching back. Exhilaration sang through her.

Master Wu and Xiao had been telling the truth. She was a dragon. Which meant there must be magic. Dragon. Magic. They were enormous words. They wouldn't settle in her mind. The concepts defied everything she believed about the world and about how she thought of herself. Or thought of Xiao. Xiao was a dragon, too. It wasn't a legend. It wasn't a dream. Dragons were real.

She had changed partly to dragon when fighting the bandit. Dragon magic had helped her be invisible while hiding from the Japanese. How else could she explain these things?

One moment she was racing forward, the next moment she was levitating just above the snow. That didn't feel right. Thought became action. She instantly touched the snow on all fours.

All fours. Four legs. She turned her head to look again at her back feet and the long, snake-like body of scales. Each scale the color of deepest midnight lightened until it ended in a silver point at the tip. Her body stretched back a dozen feet—no, two dozen feet. Or more.

Dragon.

One word changed everything. She stopped running and held very still, trying to let the idea sink in.

She wished she could tell Aunt Lu.

Then another thought. Did Aunt Lu know? Grandfather? Wouldn't they have said something?

She was tired; her heart hadn't stopped its frantic beating. Telling herself to sit, her rear legs relaxed, and her front ones curved under her chest like a cat's. The snow melted under her belly all the way back to the tip of the tail.

Her shoulder throbbed, reminding her of the tiger's attack. Three long lines were cut through her scales, pulling them out of place, and blood oozed from the two wounds that appeared to be deepest. She tried to touch the wound, but her front legs were too short to reach that high. Her claws were powerful, but they didn't work like fingers. So much to learn. The pain in her shoulder pulsed. She needed to go back to the monastery, but her body, either dragon or human, was too wobbly to take her.

Exhaustion overwhelmed Kimi. A ripple started along her chest, spread to her tail, and rose to her head. Her heart thudded within her dragon breast. Magic!

Another ripple passed through her body. The air around her grew misty—an opaque white fog illuminated the silvery glow. Inside the cloud, blue sparkles danced until her surroundings had become suffused with sapphire. The spinning stopped before she took another breath. Suddenly she found herself standing in the path, clothing restored, fully in her human shape. Her chest hurt as cold air filled her. Her body was weak, small, vulnerable, and pathetic.

Oh, no! This isn't what she wanted. She sat down and drew her knees up to her chest, pulling her shredded jacket across her body to keep warm. Still, the cold pierced her skin and settled frozen inside her bones. Her shoulder pulsed with her heartbeat.

She desperately needed to get back to the monastery and be on her way to Wen's farm, but not by walking through drifts up to her thighs. She looked at her hand and willed it to change back to a dragon claw. It didn't. Maybe it never would. The thought filled her with dismay. Her dragon self had been so powerful, so invigorating. She felt ashamed that she wanted the magic she'd always denied.

Perhaps the magic would come back. Knowing she could transform might be the trick to doing it again. Again, she willed her hand to transform, and again it didn't. Kimi rose, shaking out her limbs. She looked behind her. She had run so fast that she was now far away from the monastery. Going forward to find the road would be the shortest distance.

Fired with determination, Kimi made steady progress, sucking on fistfuls of snow to soothe her dry throat. The sky had cleared, giving her a clear sense of direction. In the late afternoon, the long rays of red-gold light shone between the tall spines of ancient trees. The sun spilled on the clear patches of snow.

When it became too dark to walk safely, she found a tight cluster of bushes and wedged herself between their branches. Dismal thoughts snuck in at the edges.

At first, the idea of having a dragon body had felt amazing. The legends and myths made the life of dragons seem marvelous—they danced among the clouds, traveled from place to place in a fraction of normal time, passed unseen among people.

If the legends were true, Xiao hadn't been lying. He really could travel from place to place at almost the same time merely by wishing it. How far could he go? And how long did it take? Could he get to Hong Kong? Or Shanghai? Did he get tired when he traveled? Changing into dragon form and then back again had sapped all her strength. Would it always be like this?

How much would she change? Would she be able to have children? Even if she could, would they be able to take dragon form? If dragons could live a thousand years, how long would a half-dragon live? Were there any other dragons left?

A shiver broke her thoughts. Her job right now was to survive the night in the snow. This time there wouldn't be a stable boy to rescue her. Tomorrow she would find the road to the monastery and make Xiao take her to Hachi. If she hadn't run away in a panic, she and Xiao would already be on their way to him. If the boy died, she would always blame herself.

* * *

In the middle of the night, Kimi slipped into a vision.

She stood in a fruit grove. It was summer, and the fruit was so ripe the orchard was filled with the honey-sweetness of fresh peaches. A slight breeze fluttered the leaves so they rang like chimes. A cloud of butterflies lifted from the branches of the trees. The sun glowed through their yellow and violet wings, sending colored lights to float to the ground like petals.

The path led across an arched garden bridge. It stopped at the edge of a pool that held an island with a white jade pagoda on its crown.

The beautiful Goddess, Kuan Yin, stood in front of the pagoda dressed in a creamy silk gown that fell in ripples at her feet. Her sleeves hung in soft folds that touched the ground. She carried an urn in one arm, tipped so that a clear stream of water spilled into the pool. In the other hand, Kuan Yin held a willow branch. Her face glowed like a pearl, and her hair coiled, exposing a slim ivory neck.

The Goddess spoke softly. "Welcome, child. I have been waiting for you."

"I'm sorry I doubted you," Kimi said, bowing low.

"It is over now," the Goddess said. "You are safe."

"Safe? I don't think any place is safe anymore."

"Yes, but you can remain apart from the world's unrest if you choose."

Kimi squared her shoulders and glared. "I cannot live contented in the mountains while people are dying."

"No, I do not suppose that you can."

"But how can I help? Until a few hours ago, I didn't believe in magic or dragons. I don't know how to help."

"You have courage, Daughter. Let Xiao help you. You will know what to do when the time comes."

"Why do you speak in riddles? Let Xiao help me do what?"

"I cannot look ahead and see the future. But I can see the shape of things before the stars turn. I know that you have a great destiny and that with Xiao's help you can accomplish wonders. Your mother would be proud of you."

Kimi's tongue felt thick, and her words trembled when she spoke. "My mother, please tell me about her?"

Kuan Yin laughed—the sound of a lightly plucked pipa with silk strings. "You are much alike, you know. She, too, had courage, and much sorrow. Ask Master Wu for her tale. Except for your father, Wu knew her best."

A mist began to rise from the pool. Kuan Yin bent to touch the back of Kimi's hand with the tip of the willow wand, and Kimi felt warmth spread through her body. For a brief moment her shoulder quit hurting. The mist swirled and shielded the goddess. Kimi seemed to move through the night sky on a cloud.

She woke as a ray of sunlight found its way through the leaves of the bushes. She raised one hand to cover her eyes. Pain flared across her shoulder. Her other hand clutched the medallion on her chest. The warmth of the medallion filled her with joy. There had been something about her mother…but the memory of the dream sputtered and died.

An icy breeze rustled the leaves overhead. A puff of frigid air blew down her shirt, quenching the fire of the medallion. She needed to move to stay warm.

Kimi scooped enough snow to clean her shoulder. The wound was hot. *Fàng pì!*

Then she noticed the back of her hand. As she remembered the vision, warmth spread through her once again.

With her willow wand, Goddess Kuan Yin had etched a small, blue lotus blossom faintly just above her wrist.

Joy swelled within Kimi. There was a Goddess, and her visions had been real.

Chapter Twenty-One

Kuan Yin hurried off to see Lord Yama, God of Death and Rebirth, but held little hope of freeing Tuan's spirit. Lord Yama ruled his realm with a fist of stone, and it was unlikely she could bend his heart.

When Kuan Yin arrived in the anteroom of the great God of Death and Rebirth, Lord Yama's clerk attended on her immediately. Dozens of hopeful souls mingled, waiting for their turn on the Celestial Wheel of Life. Those destined for the depths of Yama's Hells had already been dispatched.

Lord Yama's clerk bowed deeply. "You have not visited here for many years. How may I be of assistance?"

"I seek a man, Tuan, who was remanded to you for reincarnation. Should he remain among those souls who still wait, I wish to intercede on his behalf."

"I will review the records, though do not assume that my Lord will release him to you," the clerk replied. He went to his orderly bookcase of ledgers and removed one.

"Ah, here," he said. "The man you seek stepped on the Wheel of Rebirth not two days ago. His soul is again in the domain of living humans."

Kuan Yin grieved for Shi-lin's loss. Even if they could be reunited, Tuan would no longer remember his life with Shi-lin.

"Can you tell me where his soul now resides?"

"I know only that it is in the North along the Black Dragon River."

* * *

So far, the woods had been quiet. Only the crunch of Kimi's boots in the snow disturbed the stillness. It was the same absolute silence she remembered hiking up the mountain. But this time, the forest seemed to be listening, waiting.

When men's voices sounded ahead, she stood as still as a tree. She hoped it might be the monks searching for her, but the voices were wrong. The Japanese and their guttural barks of laughter!

Kimi moved toward the commotion, sliding from tree to tree. The woods thinned as she neared the voices. She crept forward until there were few trees left. She hid behind a broad tree nearest the road and leaned out just far enough to see the open field. Soldiers, probably from Pianshan, stood in the center of the meadow. She counted twenty men, plus the commander in his fancy jacket.

Hachi! She prayed for Wen's family to be safe. Hatred started to grow in her belly.

A trio of men wandered a short distance ahead of the others. The tallest of the trio pointed at his shorter companion and laughed. The third man bent and scooped up a handful of snow, his hat falling from his head. He made a quick ball and flung it.

How could they play? They acted like boys. She pounded her fist on the tree. These men were evil. How could they point their rifles and shoot people one day and act like happy children the next?

They were monsters. They should have heads like bears and bodies like snakes. Does the horror of their heartless rampage in Kaisun not weigh on their souls?

The leader of the party—a man with two rows of brass buttons down his chest—shouted, and the men dropped their snowballs, picked up their hats, and rejoined the rest of the soldiers clustered around the officer.

Kimi had to warn the monks!

She moved north, keeping to the fringes of the forest to avoid being seen, but she would never outdistance them climbing over branches and bypassing bushes. She ran past their current stopping place, then dashed for the road.

At the edge of the road, she lost her footing and fell into a low bush. A bare stick scraped hard into the deep cut on her shoulder, and she cried out in pain. She didn't hesitate; she rolled, scrambled to her feet, and ran again. Too late. Looking behind her, she saw two soldiers running across the meadow, their knees rising high so their feet didn't drag in the snow. Another lowered his rifle and took aim.

Panic sent her heart pounding and fueled her race to the monastery.

Kimi ran along the edge of the forest so she wouldn't be an easy target for the gunman.

She reached for the magic, but the dragon's power eluded her. She couldn't change.

Her breath started to come in uneven gasps. Her thighs burned from the exertion of lifting them clear of the snow. She looked back over her shoulder. The men with their longer legs had the advantage. By now they were almost on her.

Kimi felt their hands on her back as they shoved her face down into the snow. She tried to get up, ragged breaths tearing at her throat, then cried out as they grabbed her and jerked her to her feet, trapping her between them and the trunk of a tree.

Kimi hung like a limp doll between them—too dizzy from pain to do more than lift her head feebly. The buckles of their belts, shining orbs of a radiant sun, wavered dark and light in her pain-dimmed vision.

One soldier twisted her injured arm. He laughed, pointing to the weeping wound as his companion pulled her away from the tree and grabbed her roughly from behind. The first soldier let go of her injured arm, grabbed her around the chest, and squeezed until she thought her ribs might break. She screamed and beat at his arms.

A fire ignited in her. Her vision steadied. The man's eyes roamed over Kimi's body, and a leering smile spread across his face. His even, white teeth parted to show the tip of a pink tongue. He leaned forward, his mouth puckered for a kiss. The thought of him touching her mouth sickened her. She raised her arm to push him away. That made him laugh, and he reached to grab her face between his hands.

Pressure built behind her eyes, stiffening her jaw. Magic surged. Despite the agony she stood taller and squared her shoulders. She wouldn't let these men hurt her. Men like these killed Grandfather and Aunt Lu. They had ruined her home. They would take no more from her.

A showering of blue sparkles showed at the edge of her vision as the magic overtook her. The change began with her hands. The fingers that had pushed against the soldier's chest became talons. Her palm spread until the claws spanned his chest. She thrust him away with easy strength. His face lost all its color. His eyes bulged like a frog's. His mouth opened and closed like a fish, but only a high-pitched whine came out. Then the light left his eyes, and he fell to his knees, toppling onto his side. Fainted or dead, she didn't know or care.

Kimi looked back at her body. The transformation was complete. Blue scales covered her arms except where the shoulder was torn and gouged. She could feel energy race through her, and the pain faded.

Her bulk was double the size of the remaining soldier, and she pressed him hard against the tree trunk. He gasped for air and weakly punched her until his struggles ceased.

The need for vengeance swelled. She rose from the ground and flew toward the rest of the troop. Clawed arms reached out before her, and great jaws opened to make a deafening roar.

Some of the soldiers dropped to their knees and covered their ears. Some turned, pointing wildly back down the road the way they had come. But with a sharp command from their leader, the remainder formed two sloppy lines and lifted their weapons.

The guns angered her even more. She remembered the neat hole in Grandfather's forehead and the blood that had mingled with the broken jars of peaches where her aunt had lain. She flew straight at the soldiers. One man shot, then another, but their bullets missed. Let them shoot. She would see them in Hell before letting them pass.

Kimi swooped down and grabbed a man in her claws, digging into his shoulder and chest. His round cloth cap fell away. She heard his bones break and smelled the sudden odor of urine and feces as he soiled himself. As she rose with him, her eye fastened on the red braid that circled the cuff of his dark blue jacket. The colors were vibrant, almost alive, in her dragon's eyes. She could see the threads that wove through the braid and the ribbon of blood that flowed down his arm. He screamed and flailed, but her grip stayed firm. Men below shrieked. Some broke ranks and ran towards the woods. The others crouched, aiming their guns.

Crack. Crack.

She flung the man's body at the cluster of soldiers below. They scattered like leaves in a storm. More raced toward the forest entrance, abandoning their packs.

She dived toward the escaping soldiers.

More gunfire. Crack. Crack. Crack.

Pain grazed Kimi's side in a fiery line. She ignored it and grabbed another man, lifting him high into the air. A double row of brass buttons glinted in the sun. Their leader! On his orders the soldiers killed.

The soldier's eyes bulged, his face grew red, and his voice pleaded in words she did not care to understand. Inflamed rage filled her body with power. Rising higher, she dropped him in the path of another soldier racing toward the forest. The man landed in the snow and blood sprayed the snow around him.

A fleeing soldier changed course and headed for another gap between the trees. Kimi scooped him up, her claws tearing through the man's belly. His intestines burst from him, blue and twisted like grub worms. Putrid air seared her nose, and she tossed him aside.

Killing fed her anger. By ones and twos she hunted them down. With every death, she felt a surge of victory.

Only two soldiers remained, both sprinting away through the trees. She flew low between the trees. Her blood boiled. Each angry thought gave over to action. Chasing the two men, she unleashed mighty roars.

She grabbed the man nearest and tossed him aside.

A laugh rippled through her, its sound deep and savage.

The last soldier ran into the densest part of the forest. The spaces between the trees were now too narrow. Fate had granted this one soldier a reprieve. With the last scream of beastly rage, she turned and flew back to the meadow.

When she saw the crumpled men lying in the blood-spotted field of snow, the seething hate fled.

Spent, she settled onto her feet near the center of the field.

A tingling ripple cascaded from head to tail, and she reverted to human form, leaving her shivering in the snow. The magic folded its petals and receded from Kimi's mind. She closed her eyes and drifted into a cloud of nothingness for a moment. She didn't have the energy or the desire to cross the meadow on foot.

When she opened them again, her arms were human arms. Her arms and legs were covered in gore and blood. Bright red. As red as the braid on the soldiers' sleeves. Was any of this blood hers? She leaned over and saw the rents in her jacket. Her shoulder bled again. Through a rip in her jacket, blood flowed crimson along her ribs, a slow cascade down the side.

Kimi's knees gave way, and she collapsed in a heap, burying her head in her lap.

Her mind darted away from the images. The stench of the soldier's ruined bodies clung to her. She covered her head with her arms to quiet the screams echoing in her mind. Numbness crept over her. Awareness of the world grew smaller and smaller until she was completely inside herself.

Chapter Twenty-Two

Kuan Yin did not return immediately to Shi-lin to bear the sad news. She knew Shi-lin's heart would rest more easily if Kuan Yin could tell her of Tuan's new life.

So Kuan Yin went to Heilongjiang Province and followed the course of the Black Dragon River. She visited each family with a newborn babe, seeking the spark that was Tuan's soul.

She found the essence that was Tuan in a small town. He was the son of a butcher. Kuan Yin disguised herself as an old woman and went among the townspeople, gathering information regarding the butcher and his family.

Content that Tuan was among those who would love and care for him, Kuan Yin traveled back to the dragon heaven to speak to Shi-lin.

When the goddess appeared, Shi-lin flew to her side. "Have you found Tuan?"

"Yes, I have found him."

Shi-lin dared to hope until she saw Kuan Yin's grim countenance.

"He has ridden the Wheel of Life and is reborn," the goddess said.

If Shi-lin's heart could be broken any further, it was broken then.

Kuan Yin watched Shi-lin, hoping that she would grow to accept Tuan's passing. But after several months, Kuan Yin knew that Shi-lin's grief would know no end. For Shi-lin, heaven was not a release to paradise, but a prison locking her away from all that mattered to her.

It was then that Kuan Yin conceived a plan.

* * *

Kimi wasn't sure how long she stayed crouched in the wet snow, but it seemed to have been a long time. She found it hard to lift her drooping eyelids. She stood slowly, stiff with cold. Frozen blood still coated her arms, legs, and jacket. The odor turned her stomach.

Flecks of bright gold glimmered above the trees. The bright cloud of sparkles resolved to the shape of a dragon that dropped from the sky to hover at the edge of the meadow. Dancing motes of gold and a rainbow of green rippled down its long body—a cascading prism of hues as yellow as new bamboo shoots which deepened to emerald so rich and dark it almost appeared blue.

The dragon stopped in front of Kimi still suspended over the trampled and bloody snow.

Kimi stared in wonder. Nothing had ever been so beautiful. And so terrifying. She didn't want to imagine a screaming man dangling from those claws or see those powerful shoulders toss a body aside without effort. The thoughts chilled her, but she couldn't take her eyes off the creature's graceful majesty.

The dragon's thick neck supported an impossibly large head. Eyes like orange moons rose high to the side of each cheek. Rope-like horns—thin, twisted spirals of bone—curved over the dragon's back. A row of gleaming ivory teeth angled in toward the ruby tongue. Thick, black lips pulled back in a frightening grimace.

She felt small and exposed—a mouse in the shadow of a hunting cat. Her heart beat wildly, and the urge to run was unbearable. Though she willed her body to change, she could not transform. Could it be Xiao? The thought didn't make her less afraid. Had she been as terrible to behold? She understood why the terrified soldiers had run from her. Those who stayed to face her had been stupid with courage to think she was afraid of their guns. How could they believe such a monstrous beast would grant mercy?

How could she believe it?

Walking on air as though there were a solid path beneath its claws, the beast sank lower until its forward legs touched the ground, and as they did, the dragon's body slowly dissolved into a glittering mist. Xiao stepped out of the haze and took the last few steps to where she stood. His arms reached for her.

She retreated a few steps, her mind a swirl of anxiety.

He closed the gap between them. Touching her shoulder he said, "You're hurt."

His eyes scanned the gory field before his fierce glare returned to her. She extended a hand toward him, willing him to understand. He had to know what she'd done.

"I..." Kimi's voice came out in a hoarse croak. She swallowed and began again. "I did this." The words were dredged from her soul with difficulty. "They caught me. I couldn't get away."

Gathering her courage, she looked straight at him. His eyes didn't tighten in anger. It didn't make sense. He should be horrified by what she'd done.

He reached for her again. A large warm hand spread across her back while the other nestled her head into the hollow between his chest and shoulder. His thumb brushed Kimi's cheek; his fingers smoothed her hair.

At first she stiffened, fighting the pain, resisting the comfort he offered. Then he kissed the top of her head. Stepping back, he lowered his arms, trailing his fingers down her arms and then caressing her hands.

"You are hurt. Let us go back to the monastery." The sound rumbled through his ribs like the purr of her orange cat.

"I didn't have to kill them. I could have flown away."

"No. It took strength and courage to do what you did— two things you have always had. I love you, Kimi." He tipped her chin up with his fingers, his smile as soul-deep as his calmness.

But then he tensed. "I will keep my promise to you. If you don't wish to marry…" The pain in his voice sounded so deep she could almost touch it.

He brushed the hair that had fallen across her forehead and guided the ends, weaving them into the loose remnants of her braid. "These soldiers would have shown no mercy to the monks. You saved me the trouble of killing them myself. If they had hurt you …" Anger tainted his words.

"Dragons are not gentle, Kimi. Especially when threatened. The gods created us to punish and protect."

"Are there others like us?" she asked.

Xiao looked up at the treetops as though her question would draw other dragons near. "No other half dragons of our generation. And the full dragons? They don't care enough. They measure time differently than we do."

Xiao touched Kimi's shoulder where the tiger's claws had shredded her jacket, leaving furrows that oozed with yellowish liquid and blood. "You need to see Master Wu to clean that wound."

When she swiveled her head, pain shot up from the new wound on her ribcage, and she reached for it. Her hand came away wet with fresh blood.

"A gun, I assume." He lifted her gently into his arms.

Kimi's pain drew gray edges around Xiao's face, and his voice sounded far away. One last conscious thought echoed in her mind. Hachi.

*　*　*

When Kimi awoke she was back at the monastery. Her thoughts skittered as she folded back the blankets and sheets. The flight, Xiao's gentle arms, the Japanese soldiers. They had come from the south. How much time had passed since then?

Hachi!

Her ribs burned. Pain stabbed her shoulder as she reached across to feel her injuries. Nothing but bandages. No time to be injured. She struggled to put shoes on, one-handed.

After a knock, Xiao entered. Kimi stood, putting the pain behind her.

His eyes opened wide when he saw her standing. "You should be asleep. Master Wu said he gave you poppy juice. He wants you to rest and heal."

"I can't rest now. It already might be too late." She grunted, trying to tie her shoe. As she twisted to reach her shoelaces, the gash caused her to wince.

Xiao knelt, pushed her hands aside, and tied the laces. "Why can't you wait?"

"I have to go to Hachi. It might already be too late." She started to stand, but he pressed her good shoulder until she sat again.

"We will go," Xiao said. "And if all is well? Are you content with leaving a little boy under their care?"

"Hachi needs medicine…" And she needed to return with Hachi. Going to see him wasn't just about the medicine. But Xiao might not agree. Adopting Hachi would affect their lives, yet he had made the same kind of one-sided decision when he decided to be a potato farmer.

Xiao held the other shoe. "That does not answer my question."

Did he want her to beg? *Fàng pì!* "I'd hoped you would be willing to accept Hachi as a member of our household. I assumed there would be enough room. If not, I am sure there are places he and I could stay in Pianshan."

The thought of returning to Pianshan made her heart sink.

Xiao smiled. "Yes, there is room. For one person. Not for every stray you find in your travels."

His words made her seethe. "Hachi is not a stray. He's an orphan, like me. If that's what you think, he's better off staying with Wen." Kimi slumped back onto the bed. She couldn't undo years of longing for the mother who'd left her. She couldn't replace Hachi's mother, but when he sobbed in the night, she could hold him and let him know she cared.

"Where does this family live?" Xiao asked. His neutral expression didn't hide the glint in his eye.

"Near Pianshan. The children might be out there alone— alone with their dead…"

Xiao took on a business-like demeanor. "And how do you plan to get there in your weakened condition?"

Hope trickled into Kimi's thoughts. This time it was she who smiled. "I'm not sure I can transform, so I hope you will take me. The same way you brought me here. Let's go!" She got to her feet, trying to hide a wave of dizziness.

Xiao nodded. "Of course."

Kimi bundled up while Xiao collected a winter coat for Hachi, the medicine, and a cash gift for Wen's family. They met outside the refectory and took the long stairs down from the monastery, following the path to a small opening behind the stable. A ring of tall trees surrounded a clearing big enough for several dragons to come and go. Trying to ignore her pain, she hurried to the middle of the glade, turned, and put her hands on her hips, waiting for him to catch up.

Xiao laughed at her eagerness.

Kimi felt his warmth as he came to stand beside her. His fresh breath smelled like clothing that had been dried in the morning sun—earthy and clean.

As Xiao swept Kimi up in his arms and cradled her, a pulse of warmth went through her body. She embraced the bundle of coats, blankets, and medicine against her belly and waited for his transformation to dragon form.

Glinting speckles of gold surrounded them. Magic rippled as his body changed into the beautiful and deadly being she'd seen the previous day. Now, instead of arms holding her, she was pressed against his chest, nestled between his long front claws in a gentle, protective cage.

Only the soft tremors of his body separated the dragon Xiao from the human Xiao. As a man, he was serene. As a dragon, he was powerful.

Kimi stroked the silky scales on his chest. They were pliable, soft and feathery. Her heart slowed to match the rhythm of his beating beneath her, building between them a tonal harmony so compelling, so magical, that not even the gods could break its spell.

Chapter Twenty-Three

Kuan Yin went straight to the Court of the Jade Emperor, first among all the gods, to negotiate on Shi-lin's behalf, for only one option remained that would put Shi-lin's heart at rest. And that path was guarded by the Jade Emperor himself. Only he had the authority to settle such a weighty matter as the fate of a dragon's soul.

Kuan Yin was kept waiting in the Jade Emperor's antechamber while he judged matters of great importance and little consequence. When she was called to present her petition, she bowed deeply, knowing that the Jade Emperor, supreme among the gods, loved flattery and kowtowing.

"Heavenly Lord," she said. "I present to you a trivial matter. One of so little significance it does not merit but a moment of your time. While it may be a small matter, it is one only you can judge."

The Jade Emperor looked at her thoughtfully for the merest of moments, then he frowned. "If it is of so little importance, why do you trouble me with it?"

"Imperial Holiness, a dragon soul known to me wishes to be with her deceased husband who is human."

He raised one eyebrow. "I cannot undo death. Surely you know this. And I care little for the fluttering of human hearts."

"Kindest Master, I am glad to hear this. Will you then sign the proclamation that will give this dragon a human soul?"

The Emperor sputtered. "You did not say she wished to be human. Being with him in spirit is not enough?"

"Divine One, she wishes to join him, not observe his life from afar. Before fate can strive to bring them together, she must first be born as a human."

"She would abandon her immortal home in heaven and the magic in her soul for a human of no consequence?"

"I believe so, Mighty Ruler."

He flicked a finger at his scribe and shook his head. "So be it."

* * *

It was late morning before Kimi found the road that led to Wen's farm. They landed in a nearby clearing where Xiao changed back to human form.

Kimi's heart raced when they turned down the narrow path between the tall hedges to Wen's house. Not a breath of sound. Even the leaves in the trees in the orchard were still.

The front yard was empty. The farmhouse, pink in the late afternoon sun, had the door open, and the crate Biyu used as a seat had been knocked over.

"Wen. Biyu. Hachi. Is anybody there?" Kimi called.

A moving shadow at the doorway turned toward them. And right behind the shadow, a smaller one.

"Kimi, is that you?" Biyu asked.

Hachi stepped clear of the door. "I knew you'd come back for me!"

Biyu caught his arm before he raced across the yard. "Go get your shoes."

Kimi released the breath she held. They were alive!

When Hachi returned with his shoes on, she raced to the door and caught him up in her arms. "Hachi…" Silent tears slid down her cheeks.

"Biyu, I'm glad you're safe." Kimi nodded towards Xiao. "This is Xiao. Wen and the children, are they safe, too?"

Biyu patted her chest. "You scared me. I thought the Japanese were here again. Yes, the children are safe. Kimi, how can this be?"

Kimi hated to lie, but she saw no other choice. "Xiao found me half-frozen on the road. He took me into Pianshan to buy a coat and a proper hat. We also got the medicine for Hachi."

"When did the Japanese come here?" Xiao asked.

"Several days ago. We hid when we heard the soldiers on the road. Wen has taken the children into the fields each day since then. Hachi stays with me. His fever is gone, but he tires quickly. Did you see any soldiers on the road?"

"No, I don't think they will return," Xiao said. "The ones who took this road are dead."

Biyu frowned and tilted her head, a question in her eyes. "Won't they send others after them?"

Kimi remembered the one soldier who had escaped, terrified. Word would spread about monsters in the mountains. Neither he nor his friends would return.

"I don't think so, but it's good to be cautious," Xiao said.

Kimi took the bottle of medicine out of her pocket. "I have the medicine you suggested."

"Let me get some water," Biyu said.

"I'll get it." Kimi set Hachi down and went into the house. He trailed after her, Biyu following not far behind. Kimi pulled a pouch of money from her pocket and dropped it into the rice bucket in the kitchen. Biyu wouldn't find it until they were gone.

"Here, let me get a cup," Biyu said, following Kimi into the kitchen.

Kimi took the cup from Biyu and, following Master Wu's instructions, measured carefully and added water from the cask under the counter.

When Hachi finished taking the medicine, he went back to his mat and retrieved something. Standing, he held out the magic rock to Kimi. "I knew you'd come back."

Kimi's breath caught.

"He's been asking several times a day when you were returning. He had no doubts you were coming," Biyu said.

Kimi reached into her pocket and retrieved the companion to Hachi's stone.

He touched it with the tip of his finger. "Just like mine."

"Yes it is." Kimi brushed stray hairs from his face. She straightened and looked at Biyu. "I can't thank you enough. We need to be leaving soon."

Biyu nodded, and the three of them returned to the yard in front of the house. She righted the crate and took her seat with Hachi standing next to her.

When Wen and the children had arrived, Jai-Li and Zhong ran over to Kimi and tugged at her sleeves. "You came back," Jai-Li said.

"You've come for the boy, then?" Wen asked, his face downcast.

Wen's son looked worried. Kimi wasn't surprised when he came to stand protectively at Hachi's side.

"Yes, we hoped to take the boy home with us," Xiao said, "assuming he wants to come."

Kimi introduced Xiao to Wen and then kneeled in front of Hachi. "Do you want to come live with me? You can stay here if you'd rather. Wen has a nice house, and you will have a brother and a sister. I can't promise you will ever have a brother or a sister. Our life will be very different."

"I want to go home." Tears streamed down his face.

They pricked Kimi's eyes, too. She stroked his hair and kissed him on his cheek. "We talked about this before. Home is gone. When people die, they go away forever. Our loved ones are in the gods' care now. We have to make a new home. Both of us do. I've chosen to make my home with Xiao. We would like for you to come with us."

Hachi twisted and looked at Wen.

"It's your choice," Wen said. "Only you know what's inside your heart."

What a terrible choice to give a child! Would Kimi have chosen to go with her mother if she had returned, or stay with Grandfather?

Hachi looked back at Kimi, his black eyes wide and hopeful. "If I go with you, can I come here and visit?"

Wen joined the group at the door and touched Hachi's head. "Of course you can."

"Then I want to stay with Kimi."

Happiness filled the Hachi-place in Kimi's spirit.

* * *

The shadows were long when Xiao led them to a spot well off the road and set the boy down. The clearing, nestled between boulders and trees and not visible from the road, had gotten cold. Hachi's cheeks turned into bright pink circles.

Kimi squatted so his eyes were on a level with hers. "Do you remember how brave you were when we traveled to Pianshan?"

He nodded.

"Do you think you can be brave like that again?"

He nodded, but his eyes grew wide.

"I will tell you a secret. It's a very big secret, but I know you won't tell." She bent close to his ear. "Xiao is a dragon."

Hachi stepped back, and if Kimi didn't have a firm hold on his hands, he would have run. Instead, she pulled him closer to her and cuddled him.

"I will keep you safe. The dragon won't hurt you."

Xiao also squatted but stayed an arm's length back and held out his hand. Kimi set Hachi's warm hand into Xiao's palm.

Hachi flinched, but he didn't pull away.

"See. He's real. Just like you and me. But he's also a dragon when he wants to be. It's a long way to our house— three days at least. Xiao can take us there faster. Watch how he changes. He's big, green, and glistens with gold when he's a dragon. I will warn you, he's big and scary, but he won't hurt you. You have to be brave."

A golden mist began to fill the clearing. Even though she knew what was going to happen, her heart pounded when green sparkles caught the sun and glinted like fireflies. As the mist began to dissipate, Xiao emerged—a fearsome green dragon.

Hachi whimpered and backed so far into Kimi's embrace that she almost fell over. "It's all right. Look. I can touch him." She reached out and touched Xiao's claw.

Hachi first touched it with his fingertip, but then his little boy's curiosity took over, and he explored the feel of the claw and the scales on Xiao's dragon leg.

A bubble of lightness lifted Kimi's spirit.

He whispered to Kimi, "It's magic!"

Kimi stroked Xiao's black claw.

"Yes," she said. "It's real magic."

Chapter Twenty-Four

Kuan Yin returned to Shi-lin and presented her plan.

Shi-lin was cautious. "I would lose all memory of Tuan and of my daughter?"

"That is so," Kuan Yin confirmed.

"It is not certain that Tuan and I will meet?"

"That is also true, though I will guide your spirits where I may."

"And I will have no magic in this form?"

"You will not."

Shi-lin thought for a time. "I understand what you offer. I need time to consider."

Shi-lin thought long about what it would mean to give up her magic. Though she had not used it during the years she had been with Tuan, it had pulled at her. Memories of drifting among the clouds in the moonlight had never stopped haunting her dreams. Though she loved humans, she did not love magic any less. It also troubled her that she would lose her memories of Tuan if she followed him into the world of birth and rebirth.

If she remained in heaven, she could at least hold the happiness of their days together in her heart. She knew, though, that this happiness would be shallow without him, only a shadow of the love they had shared.

The goddess offered hope. Shi-lin knew that her heart would remember Tuan, even if memories of their prior life were gone from her mind. If their souls did not find each other in this life, they might escape the Wheel of Life and meet again in paradise--the one for human souls.

After many days, Shi-lin sent for the goddess. "I have decided to accept your kind offer. I wish it with all my heart."

* * *

Kimi watched as magpies fought over the seeds she'd scattered in the courtyard. She'd strewn the seeds over a large area, but they seemed to want to fight over the same, small patch of snow. They were rude, noisy birds, but so beautiful— gleaming white and ink-black plumage against the fresh snow.

Kimi took the first deep breath she'd taken all day. A tight knot loosened. Being a dragon changed everything. She had the power to kill, but she also had the power to save lives. An enormous responsibility. Her power could be used to help people.

She was sitting on Master Wu's favorite bench, the highest spot in the garden. From here she could see where the mountains met the sky. Between the snow-covered hills, deep, forested valleys ran along the rivers. How she'd love to soar over that ocean of white! Perhaps that was why Xiao preferred his mountain home. He could fly in the sun and wind without fear. How hard it must have been for him to be locked up inside the Imperial Palace with eyes constantly watching.

She turned at the sound of a soft step.

"May I sit with you?" Xiao asked.

Kimi slid over to make room.

He took her hands in his. They trembled when he touched the lotus mark on her wrist.

"I should have been less stern with you. I should have stayed with you. Forgive me, Kimi."

She shook her head, finally seeing the truth. "There is nothing to forgive."

Xiao lifted her gently into his lap, holding her against him like a pearl in its shell.

"You will never be alone, Kimi. Never."

* * *

Xiao had left in the morning to go make his house ready for Kimi and Hachi. She had wanted to go, but Xiao insisted he wanted to surprise her. She was mending blankets when Master Wu came in.

"Good thing Xiao is making your home ready. Maybe by tomorrow you will all sleep there. I want my monastery back." He tried to look stern, but his grin gave him away.

"What is the house like?" she asked.

"Bigger than the teahouse. You and Xiao will still have your privacy if that is your concern. Hachi can sleep in the room Xiao uses for his office. The bedroom will be yours alone."

Kimi blushed and changed the subject. "You say you knew my mother. Tell me about her, please."

He returned a gentle smile of understanding. He folded his hands in his lap. Slowly, with reverence, he began.

"Your mother was the dragon, Shi-lin, and she died of a broken heart..."

Chapter Twenty-Five

At the time apple blossoms fell to earth, and on a day when the sun lay its shadow on the moon, the dragon, Shi-lin, entered the Chamber of Rebirth.

It was there that Shi-lin was given the Elixir of Forgetfulness. Holding hope in her heart, she tasted the bitter brew.

The clerk of that Chamber guided Shi-lin to the place assigned to her on the Wheel of Life.

In that moment, Shi-lin's soul was reborn as the cherished daughter of a poor potter. His home was in a small town on the banks of the Black Dragon River.

Kuan Yin did as she promised and watched over the souls of Tuan and Shi-lin as they grew and found each other. But that is another story.

Afterword

Japan withdrew its forces six months after the massacre in Lushan and the invasion of the Liaodong Peninsula in South Eastern Manchuria.

Historians cite diplomatic reasons and mention large sums of money. Some even talk about the severe winter conditions.

As for me… I believe it had to do with the dragons.

Author's Note

One of the best parts about being a writer of fantasy is that you can stretch the truth a bit, and you get to pick the parts of history you want.

The First Sino-Japanese War in 1894-1895 is fact. The Japanese forces really did massacre thousands—60,000 by one report—leaving few survivors when they took control of Lushan (also known as Port Arthur).

Japan invaded the Liaodong Peninsula at two points— Lushan and also at Dandong. The Japanese army crossed the Yalu River between Korea and China in the middle of the night on pontoon bridges built for that purpose. The sneak attack caught the Chinese fort at Dandong entirely unaware and only four people died. It was an amazing feat of engineering and extraordinary military tactics.

As for the other parts of the story. There is no town or city known as Kaisun to the best of my knowledge in China or anywhere. Nor could I find that the massacre extended to cities other than Lushan. There is also no city known as Pianshan or a monastery at the Mountain of the Morning Song or any mountain with that name in Liaodong.

I also played with time. The defeat of Lushan was in November of 1894, not September. I wanted Kimi cold, but not that cold.

I took other liberties, more than were intentional, no doubt. Scholars of Chinese history and culture will need to forgive me. The errors are my own.

ACKNOWLEDGMENTS

Counter to popular belief, writing for me has never been lonely work. Writing is how I found myself and writing is how I found my community. Nevertheless, I cannot discount the anxiety associated with changing careers and shortly thereafter, battling cancer. I would not have found the strength and courage without my family's support. To my sister Theresa, you are my best friend and one heck of an editor. To my dad, whose glass-half-full disposition kept the sun shining even on the grayest of days. To my three daughters: Kris, Kat and Susan. You raised my spirits and kept me moving forward in your own, unique ways. You also managed to find some pretty cool husbands who did their own share of heavy lifting throughout this process. I want to extend my deepest gratitude to Carmen, Wayne, Bonny and Ana Maria. Your teaching, support, and guidance helped me realize and refine my craft. To Jen, who spent countless hours helping me through schoolwork, writing, and the never-ending process of editing. I treasured our time working together, even when it required creative and humorous methods to keep me awake. To the members of my writer's group and book club who always balanced criticism and encouragement. You inspired me to be a better writer and friend.

§

Sharon's dream was to become a published author. Our dream was to make this happen. Despite losing her battle with cancer, Sharon lives on through her writing. When Sharon retired early from her career to become a writer, we thought she was mostly crazy. However, we couldn't help but to be inspired by her perseverance and commitment to accomplish her goal. This could not have been possible without the contribution, love, patience,

care and faith of many remarkable individuals. To Martha, Amy and everyone at the Northwest Institute of Literary Arts, we are eternally grateful. Everyone poured their souls into getting Sharon through her MFA and more importantly, getting her books to print. A special thanks to Jenny and Hillel for their skills and expertise. Your eye for detail and artistic prowess helped transform a manuscript into a beautiful book. And finally, to you the reader. You have flown with dragons and learned of love, loss, and the power of imagination. You honor Sharon's memory as you read and share her stories.

ABOUT THE AUTHOR

Sharon was born in Seattle, Washington in 1952. Growing up a Navy dependent, Sharon frequently moved as a young child. Sharon finished her undergraduate studies at Central Washington University earning a B.A. in English. Later, Sharon earned an M.B.A. from City University and an M.F.A. in writing from the Northwest Institute of Literary Arts.

Sharon's career at Boeing spanned 34 years, working in the Pacific Northwest as well as the Washington DC metro area. While pursuing her own professional career, Sharon raised three daughters. Sharon had several interests and hobbies including sewing, knitting, music, and spoiling her grandchildren, the delights of her life. A voracious reader and writer, Sharon wrote several short stories and novels including the Legend of Shi-lin and Morning Song.

Proof

Made in the USA
Charleston, SC
25 July 2016